2612

FIC
FER

Ferris, Jean.

Looking for home.

# LOOKING
# FOR
# HOME

# LOOKING FOR HOME

Jean Ferris

*Farrar Straus Giroux*
*New York*

*For my mother*

# LOOKING
# FOR
# HOME

# ONE

When I was thirteen, Pop broke two of my ribs by shoving me against the kitchen counter during an argument about whether or not I could go to the movies. That was the worst thing he'd ever done to me, but far from the first bad thing. It was also what made me realize that I was the only one who was going to take care of me, and to do that, I had to get away from home and Pop's violent moods as soon as I was old enough.

Pop didn't believe in higher education for women, but I didn't care what he thought anymore. I started working my rear end off at school so I'd have good grades for college. That seemed the best way to get away from home for keeps. Later, when I was old enough, I got a job waitressing at Charlie's Dine-a-teria so I'd have the money. I also stopped trying to be the peacemaker in my family—things weren't going to change, no matter what I did—and tried instead to become as tough as nails to avoid that four-letter word, "fear," that Pop had instilled in all of us.

I couldn't understand why Mama stayed with him, much less why she'd had my four younger brothers with him. He didn't treat us kids any better than he treated her, and we all showed the effects of it. Seven-year-old Roy was often angry and sometimes cruel; Bobby and Jack, at six and five, were quiet and cautious; and Sonny, at three, was losing some of the baby enthusiasm I wished he could keep. I'd been through all of those stages myself.

As for Mama, my love for her was complicated by other feelings: pity, the mornings she cooked breakfast with fresh bruises on her face; anger, when she didn't protect me and the boys from Pop; compassion, when I saw how unhappy she was; and finally, resignation to how she was: submissive, passive, timid. I knew she loved me and the boys and that she was doing the best she could for us. But often her best wasn't good enough. That's why I had to be so tough I could take care of myself without anybody's help. I didn't want to live in fear, the way Mama and the boys did.

One of the reasons Susan was my closest friend was that she understood how it was at home, even though I couldn't talk about it. I'd been sure Susan would stop being my friend after the first time she came to my house. While she was there, Pop threw a chair across the kitchen at Bobby, who'd spilled some juice on the floor. The chair missed Bobby, and Susan had gone home immediately, white and shaken. We hadn't talked about it afterward, but we stayed friends and we both knew why she never came to my house again.

After that, she seemed to make it her job to see that I had some fun. That's probably why she arranged my meeting with Scott.

She and Tony, her steady, had included me in many of their plans since they'd started going together, two years before, when we were all freshmen. And sometimes they'd fixed me up with guys, too. But I told Susan she'd gotten the last good one; that besides Tony there were only geeks, dopes, or unattainable gods, and, once in awhile, some macho character who reminded me of Pop.

Susan said she'd prove me wrong, and one afternoon in February of our junior year, while I waited for the #3 bus to take me to Charlie's, Scott Morgan, who was, in my book, an unattainable god, and a senior as well, stopped his car and offered me a ride to work. I knew he'd just broken up with Stephanie Adams, and I knew Susan had somehow gotten him to offer me that ride, though she never told me how.

After that, he stopped for me every afternoon. He was easy to be with. Mostly, I suppose, because I let him do just about all the talking. He was good at that, telling stories and jokes, making me laugh, and pulling my waist-length, silver-blond braid, as if we were twelve instead of seventeen and eighteen. Once he told me he liked me because I was such an undiscriminating audience. It was true. When I was with him, I did laugh at almost everything he said.

I got to know him in those ten-minute rides to Charlie's, and after three weeks he asked me out.

One of the things I liked best about Scott was his disinterest in bad news. I loved the way he could ignore anything unpleasant, the way he could talk matter-of-factly about his future—summer job, college, law school—sure that it would work out just the way he planned. He always said people spoiled their good times by getting too serious.

Of course, I couldn't help noticing that he never mentioned me as a part of his future. He seemed to accept that, after his graduation, our "good times" would be over, and somehow I couldn't ask him if I had a place in his life once he finished high school. I didn't want him to think I was getting too serious and being one of those "spoilers."

After dates with him, I'd sit on my bed in the dark, my mouth tender from his excited kisses, and think about how, when I was with him, I almost forgot about life with Pop. I would rebraid my hair, which Scott had freed and tangled around us as we sat in the backseat of his car at the Quarry, and remember how he'd said he felt he was wrapping us in moonlight. And as I braided my hair, I felt as if I were binding myself back into my own world— a different, darker world than his, a world he wouldn't want to know about.

For all the kissing we did at the Quarry, Scott and I never did anything more—at least, not until the night of the junior–senior prom. It really was enough for me, that kissing, so breathless and inventive and consuming. When he told me I looked like the angel on top of a Christmas tree, I went soft in a way that scared me as well as excited me. It was impossible for me to think about being tough when I was with him.

If nobody's ever said falling in love makes you stupid, let me be the first. I was so attracted to his lack of interest in the kind of stuff that went on in my house every day that I forgot there are times you can't avoid talking about serious things if you're going to have a real relationship. But maybe I didn't forget. Maybe I didn't know it yet myself. Deep down inside, I hoped that by being the kind of girl Scott wanted, I'd get him to stay with me and his carefree world could become mine.

In late May, when I came home from Charlie's on prom night, Mama got up from the dinner table to run my bath.

"Sit down, Marie," Pop said. "Daphne's not a baby."

Mama didn't say anything. She just kept heading for the bathroom.

"It's okay, Mama," I said. "I can do it." Would this be one of Pop's explosive times, or one when, inexplicably, he let it ride? I could never predict, and didn't want to try.

"Marie!" He stood up from his chair and bellowed after her.

I heard the water splashing into the tub and Mama come back down the hall. It was partly by these occasional daring acts of defiance that I knew Mama loved me. She risked a lot by them, and I couldn't ever decide if I thought her foolish or courageous.

She sat down at the table without saying a word, while the boys watched with big, worried eyes.

Pop sat down, too, and began to eat, and Mama's shoulders, as well as mine, slumped in relief. It was Pop's monthly poker night, and he was always in a hurry to get away on those nights. Maybe that's why he let it go that time.

I hurried into the bathroom, stripped off my dirty

uniform, and got in the tub. I lolled in the steamy water and listened to my brothers running up and down the hall after dinner. I could hear Sonny calling, "Wait for me!" while Roy yelled, "Hide! Hide! He'll never find us!" There was silence for a few minutes, and then Sonny again, with tears in his voice: "Where *are* you?" Roy's teasing always made him cry, and his crying always got him in trouble with Pop.

"Open the door," Sonny cried. "I have to go potty!"

"I'm taking a bath. Use the other bathroom."

"Pop's in there. I have to go-o-o-o!"

I sighed, wrapped a towel around myself, and went to the door.

"Don't watch me," he said, coming in, his shorts already halfway off.

"Okay, but don't you watch me, either."

"Okay."

I got back into the tub and floated two washcloths strategically over me while I waited for Sonny to finish. Hitching up his shorts, he came to sit on the edge of the tub. "Hi," he said.

"Goodbye."

"Can't I stay here? They won't play with me."

"I'm trying to take a bath, Sonny. Go see Mama."

"She's smoking a cigarette in the kitchen. It smells bad."

"Oh, okay. But girls need some privacy. Put the lid down and sit on the potty."

He turned in that direction but came back. "You want my duck?" A net bag of bath toys lay on the floor next to the tub, and Sonny squatted beside it, trying to extricate a rubber duck, fussing in frustration. "It's stuck!"

"That's okay. I don't want it, anyway."

"But you *need* it." He started to cry.

Roy stuck his head in the half-open door. "Crybaby," he said.

"Am not." Sonny continued to wrestle with the duck, his face red and puckered.

"Yes, you are." Roy came into the bathroom, disentangled the duck from the bag, and held it over Sonny's head, squeezing it and making it squeak. "It's my duck now."

"Mine!" Sonny howled.

"Give him the duck and get out of here," I said, rearranging the floating washcloths. Bobby and Jack stood in the doorway, watching Sonny paw at Roy as he reached for the duck.

"Let him have it," Jack said, grabbing at the duck, too.

"Let him get it himself." Roy pranced around the bathroom, the duck in his upraised hand. Then Bobby was there, and all the boys were on the floor, fighting over the duck while it squeaked and squeaked as it went from hand to hand.

"What the hell's going on in here?" At the sound of Pop's voice, all the boys lay still and stared up at him. He looked at me. "Haven't you got sense enough to shut the door? These boys got no business in here watching you."

There was no point in trying to explain what had happened. To Pop there was no such thing as an explanation, only an excuse.

Silently, the boys got up and left the bathroom,

the yellow duck abandoned on the bath mat. Pop scowled at me again and slammed the door shut behind him. I could hear his angry voice as he followed the boys down the hall.

No matter how much I tried not to be afraid, that was always my first reaction when Pop spoke to me the way he had. As quickly as I could, I replaced that feeling with anger, indignation, indifference, anything besides fear.

The water was cool now, and scummy with soap around the edge of the tub. I got out, put on my robe, and went to my room.

On my dresser was Mama's bottle of Earthly Delights, the perfume she'd gotten for Christmas. It might as well have been gold, she used it so sparingly. A drop on Sunday before church, a few drops for the Lodge dinner, occasionally a drop to compensate for an especially hard day. And she'd left it all for me.

At first, I didn't want to use it, to take any of it away from Mama. But I knew she wanted me to, so I put some on my neck and behind my ears. Then I smoothed more in the crooks of my elbows, on my wrists, behind my knees. I wasn't going to have a life where pleasure was meted out in stingy, secret drops. I wanted happiness by the gallon.

# TWO

I waited until Pop had left for his poker game to come out of my room, all dressed in my beautiful new white dress, with my hair loose down my back. The oldest boys lay on the living-room floor and howled like wolves, and Sonny patted the hem of my skirt and said, "Daphne?"

Mama came out of the kitchen, a cigarette in her hand, to see me. "Oh, Daphne, you look like a princess in a fairy tale."

"You know you're only supposed to smoke in the kitchen, Mom," Roy said.

"I'm sorry. I forgot. Because of Daphne." She went back into the kitchen and returned without the offending cigarette.

When Scott arrived, splendid in his rented tuxedo, the boys howled again. Mama dabbed at her eyes with a tissue and practically followed us to the car.

As we drove off, Scott ran his hand through my hair and said, "You look unbelievable."

The whole evening was unbelievable. Familiar people, even Susan and Tony, looked strange in their fancy clothes. The music was too loud, the colors too bright, the air too hot. I felt giddy and a little frantic. This would be one of my last times with Scott. In two weeks he would graduate and go to his summer construction job upstate, and he still hadn't said anything about what would happen to us after he went.

So when he said, "Let's get out of here. I'm going deaf," I went without a question.

He kissed me as soon as we were in the car and then held my hand on his knee as he drove. I knew without asking that we were going to the Quarry.

"We didn't get our pictures taken," I said.

"I won't forget what you look like. How could I forget somebody named Daphne?" he asked.

"I guess I'm lucky it's not Geranium. Or Chrysanthemum."

"Daphne's a flower?"

"A little pink one. They grow on a bush. My mother loves them. I always wanted an ordinary name like Mary or Ann or Sue."

"That's no fun. Look at Scott. Every Tom, Dick, and Harry's named Scott. There's only one Daphne."

I wondered how long he'd remember that once he got to college.

The Quarry was deserted and dark, and so quiet we could hear the songs of the tree frogs all around us. Later, after the prom, there'd be other cars here, but for now it was our own.

"Did you have fun?" he asked, putting his arm around me.

"I guess so. It was sort of overwhelming."

"That's why I wanted to leave. This is better."

I lifted my hair with both hands and let it hang over the back of the seat.

"Isn't it?" he asked. "Daf?" He stroked my hair. "We can go back if you want."

"It's not that."

"What, then?"

I knew he wouldn't want to hear what I had to say, and I didn't want to have to say it, but I couldn't keep it in any longer. "I was just thinking about endings and beginnings. Wondering which we're doing."

"Why do we have to do either? Why can't we just be for now?"

When I didn't answer, he said, "I bet I can cheer you up."

He kissed me, but it just made me feel worse. When he kissed me again, I put my arms around his neck and kissed him back. I don't know if I was still hoping he'd change his mind or if I was pretending he'd never made his intentions clear or if I really was just a love-sick fool.

"Daphne. That's my girl." Slowly, he lay me across the seat and touched me, with my hair tangled in his fingers.

He held my hand on his knee again as we drove home.

"Are you okay?" he asked.

I knew he wanted me to say I was, so I did. But he never said the words I needed to hear. I wanted what had happened to change how Scott felt about me, and I knew it hadn't. I felt vulnerable, and infuriated with myself for being so stupid. Why couldn't I learn the only person I could trust was me?

I let him walk me to the door and kiss me good night on the porch. I even thanked him for taking me to the prom. Then I went inside and stood behind the screen, watching him as he went back to the car, before I closed and bolted the front door.

In my room, I took off the crumpled white dress and left it on the floor while I got ready for bed. I wanted to take a bath, but I didn't want to wake anyone. Instead, I braided my hair so tightly it pulled at my temples, and I threw my wilted rosebud corsage in the wastebasket.

The bottle of Earthly Delights was gone from my dresser.

Mama woke me up, knocking on my bedroom door. "Daphne? Are you awake?"

"No." I was surprised to find I'd slept. I had thought the furious beating of my heart would keep me awake all night.

"Scott's on the phone."

"I'm too sleepy. Tell him I'll call him later."

"Okay. When do you have to go to work?"

"Noon. What time is it?"

"Nine-thirty. You can sleep a little longer."

There was no chance that I could fall asleep again. I got up, showered, and went into the kitchen in my robe. Pop sat at the round table with a cup of coffee, reading the paper, and Mama, dressed for church, dried the breakfast dishes and doled out crackers to Sonny, who was sitting, clean and brushed, in the high chair.

"Did you have fun last night, honey?" Mama asked.

I poured myself a glass of orange juice and tried to take a cracker from Sonny's tray.

"Mine!" he squealed.

I kissed the top of his head and gave the cracker back. "It was great," I said, sitting opposite Pop at the table.

He kept reading and didn't even look up at me.

Mama extracted Sonny from the high chair. "The other boys don't want to go to church with me. They're in the yard. You can tell me all about it when you get home from work. I bet nobody looked as pretty as you."

I finished my juice and went back to my room, where I kicked the white dress into the back of my closet. As I was making my bed, I heard the phone ringing, and Pop's voice: "For God's sake, somebody answer the phone."

Are your legs broken? I thought, going to the hall where the phone was. "Hello?"

"Daphne? It's Scott. I want to talk to you about last night."

I hung up.

"Who was it?" Pop yelled from the kitchen.

"Nobody. Wrong number."

I went back to my room and got dressed for work.

# THREE

I usually liked working at Charlie's on Sundays; it meant less walking because I was stationed at the counter. When I waited tables, I was always hurrying between the kitchen and the customers, banging my hips and elbows against door frames, tables, and the counter, and raising big purple bruises. But that day I felt bruised all over, inside and out: my feelings, my body, my mind. I hated it. I'd thought I was tough, but I wasn't tough enough.

By two o'clock the lunch rush was over, and I was standing at the counter refilling napkin holders when Scott walked through the front door. I spilled a pile of napkins onto the floor and, instead of picking them up, I went through the swinging door into the kitchen.

"Daphne!" Scott called.

I heard him call my name again, but I didn't

answer. Arlene, the other waitress, came over to him, and I could hear them from the kitchen.

"What can I do for you?" she asked him.

"I need to talk to Daphne."

"I guess that's up to her."

"It's important. Can you tell her that? I'm not leaving until she talks to me."

"I'll tell her, but I think I know the answer."

Arlene came through the door into the kitchen. "Daphne, there's a boy out there . . ."

"I know. I heard him. I don't want to talk to him."

"I figured. But I don't think he discourages easy."

"I don't want to talk to him."

"Okay," she said, shrugging, and went back to the counter.

Before she reached him, Scott said, "I heard. But I'm not leaving."

"Whatever," Arlene said. She went about her business, while I stayed in the kitchen and Scott sat at the counter, drinking a glass of water.

At three Arlene said, "Can't you take a hint?"

"It's important."

"Must be."

"Please. Go ask her again to come out."

"You know the answer."

"Just ask her."

Arlene came into the kitchen. I'd spent the past hour unloading the dishwasher, refilling ketchup, sugar, salt, and pepper containers, helping Charlie make a list of supplies we needed, and trying to forget I'd ever known anybody named Scott.

"He's still out there," Arlene said.

"I don't want to see him."

"What time do you get off tonight?"

"Eight."

"You'll have to come out when the dinner crowd gets here."

"Then I'll be too busy to talk."

"Is this guy a criminal or a pervert or what?"

"No. He's just . . ." I didn't know what to call him.

"Well, whatever he is, he's sure persistent."

Okay, I thought. I've got to end this right now. "I'd better see him, then," I said.

Charlie came in from the alley, where he'd gone to dump the trash, and closed the door. "Go ahead," he said. "We're not busy. Anyway, he's been out there an hour and hasn't spent a dime. Who needs him?"

"Thanks, Charlie. Arlene, would you tell him I'll meet him out back?"

Arlene went to the counter. "Okay, loverboy, she'll meet you in the alley."

"Daphne," Scott called as he came jogging toward me. "Why did you hang up on me? Why won't you talk to me?"

I stood against the concrete wall, my arms folded. "I think I better just say goodbye to you early."

"But why? Okay, okay. I know. Maybe what happened last night wasn't such a good idea. But you didn't stop me."

"And I'm not blaming you, either. But it was a mistake." He put his hands on my shoulders, but I shrugged them off. "You're leaving in two weeks, anyway. What's the point?"

"It doesn't have to happen again, Daf. I'll forget

it if you will." He stood too close to me, but he didn't try to touch me again.

"I can't. Could you?"

"Why not? If I'd known this was how you'd feel, I'd never . . ."

"You didn't even ask me," I said, knowing I was as angry with myself as I was with him. If he'd asked me, I'd probably have done it anyhow.

"You didn't say anything." He sounded angry now, too.

"Okay," I said wearily. "We can't undo it. I wish we could. Goodbye. I hope you have a great time in college. I have to go back to work."

"Can't we be friends, Daphne? We did have fun together."

I nodded, remembering, and wishing I wouldn't. "Yes, we did."

His face brightened. "So, no hard feelings?"

"Sure," I said. He really had no idea what I was talking about.

"Okay," he said, sounding relieved. "I'll write you. Take care." He touched my arm and went off down the alley, and I went back into Charlie's.

# FOUR

School ended, but my schedule didn't change much. I adjusted my hours at Charlie's to fit around my summer-school classes—classes that were essential to my plans for college and for getting out of Seeley and away from Pop. I had to graduate in January so I could work full-time until September for my college money.

I tried to be so busy I wouldn't have time to think about Scott, but I couldn't quite manage that. I thought about him. I even missed him, but I wasn't sorry we'd broken up. My softness when I was with him had made me vulnerable and I didn't like that.

Susan was sympathetic and, I think, a little disappointed that her matchmaking hadn't been more successful. All I told her was that Scott and I had differences we couldn't resolve and that, since he would be gone all summer, and then off at college, trying to patch things up didn't seem to make much sense.

Mama, too, wondered what had happened to Scott, and I told her what I'd told Susan. She watched me closely for days after that, in the same way she watched Pop, with careful, measuring looks.

At the end of July, I was on the #3 bus, coming home from my shift at Charlie's. It was after ten and hotter than normal. My uniform was sweaty and stuck to me, and I wasn't thinking about anything except how much I wanted a shower, and how much I hoped Pop wouldn't still be up. I'd already had all the hassles I was interested in from an extra-busy night at Charlie's.

At least that's what I thought was on my mind. But somewhere deeper I must have been piecing things together—how tired I'd been for the past month or so, the intermittent morning nausea that I thought was from the same bug Sonny had had, and when had I last had my period, anyway? Suddenly all those clues clicked together, and I thought, My God, I'm pregnant.

I must have made a funny sound because the lady sitting across from me, clutching a gray sweater around her, even though it was so hot, looked at me sharply and then away.

My heart started to pound the way it had prom night, so hard I could barely get my breath. This couldn't happen to me. It would ruin all my plans. If I missed any school, or any days at work, I wouldn't have the grades or the money to go to college. If Pop found out, I wouldn't have to worry about college anymore: he'd probably knock me into next week. What could I do? I didn't want to ask for help—I wanted to be able to handle anything that happened to me all by myself.

When I stepped off the bus, my legs were shaking so hard I could hardly stand. Walking home, I had to keep stopping to hold onto something, to steady myself and gasp for air. By the time I got there I was hoping that not only Pop but Mama, too, would be in bed. I didn't see how she could miss noticing something was wrong.

Mama was alone in the living room, watching TV and drinking iced tea. "Hi, honey," she said. "Busy night?"

I sat down next to her on the couch, mostly because my knees were too shaky to keep holding me up. "Very. I don't know why. Hot weather takes my appetite away."

"Me, too. But it seems to make the boys hungrier than ever. I only get out of the kitchen when they're asleep."

"Where's Pop?"

"He went to bed early. They're pouring foundations for some new apartments at six in the morning, when it's cooler. Want some tea?" She rattled the ice cubes in her glass.

"No, thanks. What are you watching?" Normal words came out of my mouth in a normal way. I was astonished.

"I don't know. Some movie. I'm just enjoying sitting here by myself."

"I'll go take a shower, then."

"I didn't mean how that sounded, Daphne," Mama said, sitting up. "You're always welcome to stay."

"That's okay. I want to get out of this uniform, anyway. Good night." I kissed her cheek and went down the hall to my room.

Without turning on the light, I shucked off my uniform and sat on the bed in my underwear, my hands on my stomach. Somebody was in there. Who?

I took a deep breath. It didn't matter who. There was no way I could keep this baby. I was sorry I'd thought of it as a person.

I ripped the spread from the bed, pulled down the sheet, and punched the pillow furiously. Why was this happening to me? There were other girls who deserved it more than I did, girls who took chances and got away with them. Why couldn't Scott have gotten involved with one of them? I'd always been so careful, so strong, done the right things, even when they were hard. Why couldn't I be allowed one little mistake?

I lay down, still in my underwear, and thought about the dumb, dull letters Scott had written me, about building roads and drinking beer. I hadn't written back. I didn't want to. Even if I were to write him now to tell him I was pregnant, he wouldn't be any help. The most he would do was send me money. He certainly wouldn't offer to marry me. The idea was ludicrous. I wouldn't marry him if I was carrying triplets, if he was the last man on earth, if Pop put a gun to my head. I didn't want anybody else complicating this problem. I would depend on myself to take care of it—nobody else.

I took a shower and went to bed, where I lay awake almost all night, deciding what to do next.

# FIVE

By morning, I'd gotten it figured out. I had money in the bank from two years of working at Charlie's. It was my college money, and I'd sworn I wouldn't touch it, but having a baby meant not going to college as far as I was concerned. Four little brothers had taught me how hard it was to take care of a baby and try to do anything else. I wanted something more from college than what I'd already had: juggling school, work, and helping Mama with the house and the boys. I wanted freedom and choices. That meant no baby.

I would have to use some of my money to buy those things. If it meant working another few months to earn it back, and starting college later than I'd planned, then that's how it would have to be.

During the night, I'd remembered the speaker who'd come from Planned Parenthood to talk to our tenth-grade hygiene class. She'd said Planned Parenthood helped with problem pregnancies. I couldn't think of a better name for what was happening to me.

Between classes that morning at summer school I called Planned Parenthood and made an appointment for after school. Then I called Charlie and told him I'd be late to work but that I'd stay later to make up for it. I wanted to get this taken care of as fast as possible so I could feel like myself again and not like some terrified child.

It never fails to amaze me how little attention people really pay to each other. That day, I sat through my classes, dazed and blank, and the only time I was called on, I gave the wrong answer in a trembly whisper and the teacher went right on to someone else and no one even turned to look at me. Me, who almost always knew the right answer and who always spoke up.

Susan would have noticed, but she was in California visiting her grandparents. I was just as glad. I didn't want her to know about this.

At Planned Parenthood the first thing I had to do was get a pregnancy test. I told the technician it was a waste of time, I knew I was pregnant; but she did the test anyhow. Sure enough, in two minutes there was a blue spot in the test zone. I don't know why it's called a positive result when it shows you're pregnant. It felt negative to me.

Then I went in to talk to a counselor. Her name was Kerry. She wore round red glasses that made her look very alert.

I sat down and told her I wanted an abortion.

"Do you know what your other choices are?" she asked me.

"Have it or don't have it. I don't want to have it. I can't have it."

"There's another option, too," she said. "Have you considered adoption?"

"No." It hadn't even occurred to me. That meant having the baby.

"Let's talk about all these choices, then. The best way to make a decision is to consider every alternative."

It was a long interview. I told her it was unnecessary but she insisted, so we made lists of pros and cons for every choice, and though Kerry always referred to "the pregnancy" instead of "the baby," and though that's how I tried to think of it, too, I couldn't forget that this was a real person, however inconvenient, we were talking about.

Then she asked me, "How do the other people in your life feel about this pregnancy? Your partner, your parents?"

"My parents don't know about it, and I don't want them to. And my partner isn't in the picture anymore. This is up to me."

"Parents don't always act the way we think they might."

"Mine do."

"Maybe you should find out for sure. It's hard to make an educated choice when you don't know all the facts."

"Believe me, I know all the facts. Just tell me how to get an abortion."

"Let's make another appointment a few days from now, after you've had a chance to consider your options."

"I've considered them all I want to." A hot bubble of angry frustration rose in me.

"How long have you known you're pregnant?"

"Since yesterday." If I'd known about it for years, I wouldn't have changed my mind.

"I don't think there's any harm in thinking about your choices for a few more days. You've hardly had time to absorb the news, much less consider the future."

"Oh, all right." I guessed she had rules she had to follow. We made an appointment for the beginning of the next week. I knew that, no matter how much time I took, I'd never talk to Pop about it. I didn't want to think about what he'd do to me if he knew I was pregnant. As for Mama, she didn't need anything else to worry about. This was my problem to handle myself.

# SIX

That Saturday night, Pop went out to his monthly poker game. Mama and I rounded up the boys from the dark back yard where they ran, barefoot and in shorts, watermelon juice from supper dried on their narrow chests, catching lightning bugs and putting them in jars.

After we'd bathed them, read to them, and put them to bed, I took a shower and went to lie on my own bed with the lights off. I stared at the ceiling and listened to my heart. In the past few days it had often surprised me by suddenly breaking into a panicky, fluttering rhythm that caused me to stop what I was doing and wait for it to settle down. These unexpected episodes made me feel fragile and unfamiliar to myself, off-balance and wary, but no amount of resolve seemed to prevent my independent heart from doing whatever it wanted.

Mama opened the door to my room. "Daphne?" she whispered. "Are you awake?"

"Yes, Mama. What is it?"

She crept in and sat hesitantly on the edge of my bed. She wore a cotton nightgown that had been washed from blue to almost-white, with a bow hanging limply at the neckline.

"It's too hot to sleep. I just lie on top of the covers, trying not to touch any part of me with any other part. If I do, it sweats and sticks."

"I know what you mean. I was lying here doing the same thing."

A cricket sang under the open window, and my skin felt moist and glossy.

"Daphne?" Mama cleared her throat. "Daphne. You know I don't interfere with you. The way you are, I figure you've earned your privacy. But you've been so quiet all summer and so preoccupied, and I just wondered if, well, if there was anything you wanted to talk about. To me."

I was horrified to feel tears in my eyes.

Mama took my hand. "You know, when you were born, I hoped so much you would be a girl. I wanted to be everything for my little girl that my mother hadn't been for me. It was like having my own chance to get it right. Well, I guess everybody makes their own style of mistakes. I didn't know, either, that I'd have those four boys who'd take so much of my time and energy. Take it away from you, I mean. And your father . . ." She sighed. "Well, he is your father, and I was taught families should stay together."

Our hands were hot and sticky together. Tears puddled in my throat, so that I couldn't talk, and I squeezed her hand.

After a while, Mama said softly, "I had an abortion once. When Sonny was not quite a year old. I just didn't think I could survive another baby. I was so tired. I didn't tell anybody. Your father thought I was having some female problems and needed treatment for them. Do you remember that?"

I shook my head. Why was she telling me this now?

"It doesn't matter. I tried not to make much of a production of it. Anyway, the physical part wasn't what was the hardest. Every time I see a child about the right age, I think, My baby'd be that big now, and I want to cry. Maybe not everybody feels like that, but I do, even though I know it was the best thing for me to do then and I wouldn't make any different choice if I had it to do over again."

"I can see how that's a hard decision to make," I whispered. If I'd spoken any louder my voice probably would have given me away.

"Do you? Have I guessed right, then?"

The cricket sang loudly under the window.

I finally nodded. She must have known I was pregnant even before I did.

"I thought you were sick too long for it to be the flu. Oh, Daphne, what will we do? How can we ever tell your father?"

"I've no intention of telling him anything," I said. "And I don't want you to, either."

Mama hesitated and then said, "Your father's under a lot of stress and he—"

"Oh, Mama, that's nonsense. He isn't under any more stress than lots of other people who don't use their fists to solve their problems. You don't have to make excuses for him."

I sat up and put my arms around her. Through the thin gown her body felt frail and soft. She rested her head on my shoulder and rubbed my back. "Does Scott know?"

"No. It's better if you don't know, either. Then you have no secrets to keep from Pop. Don't worry. I'll be okay." I sounded confident and adult to my own ears, and, I hoped, to Mama's. But the fast, frightened beat of my heart wasn't fooled.

My shoulder was wet where Mama's head rested; I couldn't tell if it was from tears or just the pressure of hot skin.

At my next appointment with Kerry I told her, "I understand you want me to make an educated choice, and that's what I'm doing. I choose abortion. Just tell me how it works and how I can get one."

She told me then about blood tests and pelvic exams and speculums and local anesthetics, showing me everything on a chart which I'd already seen in that tenth-grade hygiene class. It had grossed me out then, and it grossed me out this time, too. None of it seemed to have anything to do with the way Scott used to unbraid my hair in the backseat of his car at the Quarry and let it tangle around us as he kissed me. But those were thoughts I didn't want to have anymore, and I concentrated harder on what Kerry was saying.

She talked about cramping and bleeding and hormone changes and sadness—things I hadn't known about. I don't know how I thought an abortion worked. By magic wand, maybe. It helped to know that Mama had been through this and I hadn't even noticed.

Kerry gave me a phone number to call to set up

an appointment. I put it in my pocket, thanked her, and caught the bus to Charlie's. I felt cold all the way to work, on a sweltering August day.

I called the number Kerry had given me and made an appointment for the abortion. The night before it was scheduled, I had hot, red, screaming dreams and woke up so shaken I called and postponed it a few days. I needed more time to feel ready.

I thought of almost nothing else all day and all night. The baby, the pregnancy, was curled inside me, cozy and oblivious to the storm it had created. Scott was far away, cozy and oblivious, too. I was alone, in the middle of the storm, trying as hard as I could not to get blown off my course.

When Roy was born, I was ten, and when Sonny came, I was fourteen. In those four years, Mama was pregnant almost all the time, and the way her shape changed fascinated me. There was somebody hiding in there, waiting to come out, and I so wanted to know who it was. I put my hand on her stomach and felt the little body roll under my palm. I put my ear against her and listened for any sound. I put my mouth to her and called, "Hello, baby."

It seemed such a strange way for new people to arrive in the world—strange and miraculous. Would I be doing a terrible thing by interrupting that awesome, slow process? Mama hadn't thought so. For her it had been the right thing to do.

I postponed the abortion again. As sure as I was about having it when I was awake, my dreams seemed to be telling me something different. I knew that by putting it off I was betraying myself and my future. I wanted to have the abortion. I was positive I did. It was the only sensible thing to do.

I stood with my hand on the phone. This time I'd make the appointment and I'd go and get it over with and go on with my life as if nothing had ever happened. My heart started its bongo act as I stood there, as if to let me know that it wasn't going to be that easy. My hand released the phone, even as I willed it not to.

Oh, damn it, I thought, furious and despairing. How can I be so weak? If only I didn't already know too much about pain and violence.

I knew I couldn't do it.

# SEVEN

E very morning, I studied myself in the mirror
to see if everything that was happening made
me look different. It seemed impossible, but I looked
about the same as always. My stomach was still
flat, though my bosom was a little bigger. The only
indication something had changed were the shadows under my eyes that showed I wasn't sleeping
well. The nausea I'd felt earlier in the summer had
abated, and returned only occasionally now, so I
felt okay except for being very tired. Whether that
was from lack of sleep or being pregnant or anxiety
or all three, I couldn't tell.

Mama watched me all the time and I was afraid
that would alert Pop that something was wrong. I
overestimated the amount of attention he paid to
her, or to me. He didn't notice a thing.

It was clear to me that, since I'd chickened out
of the abortion, I was going to have to have the
baby and give it up for adoption. At least I could

call it a baby now, instead of just a pregnancy.

And if I was going to have it, I'd need to go somewhere else to do it. There was no way on earth I could live at home with Pop and have a baby.

I wanted to make my own plans, my own arrangements, take charge again to prove that I could. I needed to know that I wasn't really weak.

I looked in the phone book for homes for unwed mothers—such an old-fashioned phrase, I thought—but found no listings. Who could I ask about such places when I didn't want anyone to know I was pregnant?

Finally, I called Kerry at Planned Parenthood and asked for the names of some homes. There was one nearby and several farther away. The near one was full and wouldn't have a vacancy for at least two months. That was longer than I could afford to wait. Two of the other ones were in the process of being converted into drug rehab residences, due to lack of use by unwed mothers. The other home required my parents' permission to admit me, since I was under eighteen, and there was no way I could ask my father for that.

I realized it didn't really matter where I went. I had money in the bank, I was hardworking and resourceful and back to being tough as nails. Those seemed all the ingredients I'd need for a successful escape. I could get a job somewhere until I couldn't work anymore, and then I'd have my savings. I'd give the baby up and decide what to do next. I could do all those things anywhere. The project seemed perfectly simple and manageable. I couldn't face then how also perfectly terrifying it was.

\* \* \*

Summer school ended and I had extra time to help Mama. I cleaned out the garage and painted the boys' rooms. I weeded the garden and made big pots of chili and spaghetti to freeze.

"Daphne," Mama kept saying, "you shouldn't work so hard."

But I couldn't stop. I wanted to do things now that would help her in the months to come. Months when I wouldn't be there. But I couldn't tell her that.

"It's okay," I'd say. "Don't worry."

Of course she kept worrying. That was Mama.

One night, while we were cleaning up the kitchen after supper, and Pop and the boys were glued to the TV in the living room, she said to me, "I'll miss you."

"I won't be going anywhere for a while yet." That was ambiguous enough, I thought.

"Whenever you go, I'll miss you," she said. "But when you go, I'll know it's because you have to."

I should have known I couldn't fool her.

I told my parents I wouldn't be able to go to Ambrose Lake with them that Labor Day weekend. I told them Charlie needed me.

I was sure they'd know I was lying, just as I'd been sure Charlie would see through me when I'd asked for that weekend off to go camping with my family, but no one said anything, though Mama gave me a long, serious look.

And Pop, of course, was furious.

"What the hell do you mean, Charlie's got to have

you? Who's going to help your mother? I've got a mind to call Charlie up myself and tell him what I think about this."

"It wouldn't do any good, Pop. Arlene's on vacation. There isn't anybody else to help. I got last Labor Day weekend off. I got this Fourth of July weekend off. It's my turn to work. I'll help Mama get everything ready on this end. I'll pack the camper for you." Anything. I'll do anything. Just don't make a stink. You and the boys could help, too, but you never seem to think of that. Finally he relented. "Okay. If that's the way it has to be. But you tell Charlie, *we* need you next year."

What happened next year was going to come as a surprise to Pop.

At noon on the Friday before Labor Day, Pop came home from work expecting, as he always did, to find the camper loaded and a picnic lunch in the cooler on the front seat, just waiting for him to slide into the driver's seat and drive away. And that's exactly what he found. I made sure. Everything had to go smoothly that day.

The hardest moment was saying goodbye to Mama and the boys. Roy, Jack, and Bobby gave me hurried pecks on the cheek and mumbled goodbyes before climbing into the camper, but Sonny wrapped his arms around my neck and cried against my cheek. Finally Mama took him, and I had to hug her with him between us.

"Be careful, Daphne," she said. "I'm sorry I—"

"I know, Mama," I said, cutting her off. "It's all right."

Holding Sonny in one arm, she took something from her pocket and put it into mine, then got into the camper.

I stood in the driveway, waving to them as they headed off down the street, glad when they turned the corner and I could stop. I refused to cry even when I found the twenty-dollar bill Mama had put in my pocket.

Then I went into my room, took the nylon duffel bag I'd used for my gym clothes off the top shelf of my closet, and began to pack. There wasn't much to take: underwear, two pairs of jeans, a skirt, some shirts. A couple of pairs of shoes. A hairbrush and shampoo. A paperback copy of *Jane Eyre*: it was on the reading list for senior English, a class I wouldn't be taking now. I stuffed the slim bundle of Scott's letters in next to *Jane Eyre*. I wasn't sure why I didn't throw them away. He hardly seemed real to me anymore.

I blotted my face with tissues and lay on my bed to cool off.

I'd slept in this bed pushed against this wall for as long as I could remember. It had never even occurred to me to rearrange the furniture. Now I was about to rearrange everything.

I got up and took the white prom dress from the closet and put it into a paper grocery sack. In the bathroom, with Mama's big sewing shears, I cut my hair off at my ears and put the long white-blond hanks into the sack with the dress. Then, with nail scissors, I cut my hair even shorter, into ragged scallops. When I finished, I took the grocery bag outside and put it in the trash can. That hair and that dress had caused me too much trouble.

I left a note propped against the pillows of my parents' bed saying that I'd gone away to live my own life. Weak as that sounded, it's all I could think of to say. Mama would understand, but Pop never would, no matter what I wrote.

My letter to Susan said the same vague things, and I felt guilty about not telling her the truth. But the fewer people who knew about this baby, the better.

Then I took the bus to the Trailways station and bought a ticket for wherever the next bus was going. It turned out to be Lincoln.

# EIGHT

I sat, sweating through my T-shirt, on the hard bus-depot bench. There hadn't been room in the nylon gym bag for my winter jacket, so I held it in my lap, where it felt bigger than it really was. I'd have left it behind, but I'd need it in a few weeks and I wouldn't have the money to buy a new one.

An announcement, loud and indecipherable, came over the speaker, and I knew, from looking at the wall clock, that it signaled the departure of the bus to Lincoln. I boarded the bus and sat down, automatically reaching for my long braid, to bring it to the front so I wouldn't lean back on it, before I remembered it was gone.

By now my parents and the boys would almost be at Ambrose Lake, about to compete for a place in the campgrounds with the other Labor Day weekend campers. I never thought I'd be remembering those trips with nostalgia: the tired and fretful little boys; Mama exhausted from trying to soothe them, glancing nervously at Pop to see how irritated he was getting; and Pop swearing and blowing the camper's horn as he sped down the highway.

Then the turmoil of trying to establish camp before it got dark, with everyone hot and hungry, followed by three days of mosquito bites, dust so fine it coated the teeth, and sitting with Mama in the warm lake shallows, playing with the boys. In the evenings, if Pop had caught enough fish, there'd be peace around the camp fire; if not, wary silences and bland conversation, trying to forestall the inevitable outburst from him, as if he blamed us for his lack of success.

I wouldn't miss that. Mama and the boys were something else, though. There'd been plenty of times I'd wished I didn't have any brothers, when they were noisy and rude and fooled around with my things. And there'd been plenty of times, too, when I was impatient and annoyed with Mama. But now home and Mama and the boys seemed familiar and appealing. I'd lived with them all for my whole life and I knew what to expect at home. I had no idea what would happen to me in Lincoln.

I had to remember that the reason I was going to Lincoln was *because* of what I could expect at home: Pop.

A girl in a flowered dress shoved a small bag onto the overhead rack and dropped into the seat beside me. "Okay if I sit here?" she asked.

"Sure."

The girl, her big hoop earrings almost lost in the frizz of her riotous red hair, lifted the hem of her dress and fanned her knees with it. She had at least one ring on every finger. "Wow, it sure is hot out there. Six hours on an air-conditioned bus isn't a bad way to keep cool, is it?"

"I guess not."

"I'm going to Lincoln to meet my boyfriend. He's stationed at Fort Hillman, and he's got a twenty-four-hour leave starting tomorrow morning. It's his first leave since he finished basic." She laughed. "There's nothing in my bag but a nightgown and some perfume, and I probably won't even need those."

My cheeks got red, and I turned to look out the window.

The girl kept talking. "I wrote to him every day. I'm telling you, it seems more like eight years than eight weeks since I've seen him. You got a boyfriend?"

I shook my head.

"Oh, well. What takes you to Lincoln?"

"I'm going to live there."

"Yeah? I've sure thought about leaving Seeley, but I don't know. I guess I'm not ready yet for the big city full-time. Maybe when me and my boyfriend get married."

I looked at her. "When's that?"

"We don't have a date yet. But I've got my promise ring." She held out her left hand. A tiny diamond winked on her fourth finger, dwarfed by the big rings on her other fingers. Her index finger even had two rings, one gold with a blue stone and the other a silver band above the first knuckle.

"It's very pretty," I said, and turned back to the window.

I thought about Scott. A promise ring is the last

thing that would have entered his mind, even if I told him I was pregnant. It was also the last thing I'd have been interested in accepting from him. Yet here I was, carrying his baby.

As the bus rushed through the countryside, the girl kept talking energetically, running her sparkling fingers through her hair, flapping her skirt, a flurry of words and motion, until I closed my eyes and pretended to sleep. Sunlight fell through the window into my lap, and after a while I really did sleep.

I woke abruptly when the bus stopped at the terminal in Lincoln. The red-haired girl was already on her feet, pulling her bag from the rack. "Bye," she said over her shoulder as she started down the aisle. Still half asleep, I took my own bag and was off the bus before I realized I'd forgotten my jacket and had to go back for it.

I stood beside the empty bus, watching people heading purposefully away. The girl in the flowered dress turned to wave as she got into a taxi at the curb and, even at that distance, her rings caught the waning daylight. I was the only one who seemed to have nowhere to go, and it gave me a lonely feeling to know that nowhere in this big city was anyone waiting just for me.

Across the street from the bus station stood a five-story stucco building with a red neon sign flickering HOTEL EDISON in the gray city dusk.

It didn't look fancy, but I couldn't afford a fancy hotel even if I'd known where to find one. Besides, I wasn't brave enough to wander around in the dark in a strange city.

I crossed the street and discovered the Edison

looked worse close up. The windows were dirty and the paint flaking. My heartbeat started galloping as I stood at the door, but since I had no better plan than opening it and going in, that's what I did.

I entered the lobby, where several old men sat on dusty-looking couches watching TV. They all stared at me as I walked from the front door to the desk, and they kept staring as I spoke to the clerk.

"What can I do for you, doll?" he asked, slicking back his oily hair with the palms of his hands.

"I need a room." My voice had a little quiver in it, but I cleared my throat and hoped he wouldn't notice.

"Just for a night?"

I didn't like the way he looked at me, but I was tired and I had to stay somewhere. I took a deep breath and said, "Yes. Just for tonight."

"Happy to have you, doll. My name's Kayo. Let me know if there's anything I can help you with." He winked. "Anything at all."

The old men kept watching me from their couches as I paid for the room, took my key, and entered the decrepit elevator across from the desk. Once in it, I leaned against the wall, trembling. Was I doing something monumentally stupid?

The elevator jerked to a stop on the fourth floor. A thin dark red carpet ran down the hall, worn threadbare in front of each door.

A wave of stifling hot air rolled out of the room when I opened the door. As soon as I'd thrown my duffel bag, purse, and jacket on the bed, I wrestled the window open. That's the only air-conditioning I was going to get at the Hotel Edison.

The effort left me dripping and shaky. I went into

the tiny bathroom, the floor and walls covered with white hexagonal tiles, and splashed water on my face and throat, not bothering to dry myself with one of the thin towels. The cool water sliding down my neck and into the top of my T-shirt felt wonderful.

The room and bath looked clean enough, despite the spare wooden furniture and the rust stains in the sink and tub. I wedged a chair under the door knob and dropped into the hollow in the center of the bed, letting the small breeze that puffed at the limp curtains dry the moisture on my face. Tomorrow I would find a YWCA and move in. It had to be safer than this.

It was dark outside the window now, and the traffic sounds were loud. In spite of the street noises, my long nap on the bus, and straining to hear any suspicious sounds outside my door, I disappeared again into sleep.

# NINE

I woke up in the dark and it took me a minute to understand why my bed felt unfamiliar and the air in my room smelled stale, like old cigar smoke. When I opened my eyes, I saw the intermittent neon glow of the Hotel Edison's red sign at the open window and heard the grind of gears from a car on the street below.

I turned on the light and looked at my watch: four o'clock. I pulled off my wrinkled clothes, hung them in the closet, turned out the light, and dropped again into the hollow in the thin mattress, where I lay, listening once more for sounds—footsteps, breathing, a key in my lock. Everything in this place is too thin, I thought as I finally fell asleep: the carpet, the towels, the mattress, the walls. Too thin for protection. Too thin for comfort.

When I woke in the morning, I could already feel the heat building in the room, and I was starving. I decided I needed to eat breakfast before I looked for the YWCA. I showered and dressed, and left my room. Kayo was still at the desk. The old men watched cartoons on TV. I couldn't tell if they were the same old men from the night before or different ones.

"Going somewhere?" Kayo asked me.

"Breakfast," I said, not looking at him.

"You don't want to eat around here, a good-looking girl like you," he said. "Go uptown about three blocks. It gets nicer. There's a couple coffee shops up there. I'd take you myself if I wasn't on duty."

"That's okay," I mumbled, pushing open the front door.

"Hurry back, doll," he said, slicking back his hair.

Once outside in the daylight, I felt safer than I had last night, but I could see what Kayo meant. Three men, one without a shirt, squatted on the sidewalk, their backs against the Hotel Edison's wall, arguing. They stopped when they saw me, and stared, the same way the old men in the lobby had. Across the street were the bus station and a bar, and farther down the block, an adult bookstore and a tattoo parlor. A man with a shaved head waited in front for one or the other to open.

I shivered, even though it must have been eighty degrees already.

I went into the first coffee shop I came to, and sat at the counter. At Charlie's, that's where people alone usually sat. People with companions wanted a table or a booth. I ordered a huge comforting breakfast: pancakes, eggs, sausage, toast, and juice.

While I waited for it to come, I made calculations in my head, trying to determine how long I could be without work, either now or later. It didn't seem like very long. How much did it cost to have a baby? Where would I find a doctor? Could I really do all this by myself? By the time my breakfast came, I was thinking reluctantly of home. If I went home anytime before Monday night, everything could be undone. Pop would never know I had been gone. I'd still have my job at Charlie's. Maybe I could still have an abortion.

No. I knew I couldn't do that. I had no choice but to stay. I sighed. So I'd better get busy and find the Y. Then I'd have the weekend to explore Lincoln. Tuesday I'd look for a job and a clinic for prenatal care.

After breakfast, I decided to take a quick look at downtown Lincoln. Kayo was right. The city's character changed about three blocks from the hotel. The stores were nicer, the streets cleaner, the office buildings taller and more modern. Here and there a shop was being remodeled.

Saturday shoppers passed me, looking decisive and purposeful, and I envied them. They knew where they were going, and I felt aimless and lost.

On the way back to the hotel, I bought a newspaper and a city map at a newsstand. When I asked to borrow the hotel's phone book, Kayo invited me into the office so he could help me look up whatever I wanted.

"Thanks, I can do it myself," I told him as his heavy hand covered mine on top of the book. I pulled the book and my hand away from him and went to stand by the elevator, listening to it clank interminably down to me while Kayo called, "I can come up and help you. Always glad to be of service to a lady. Anything you need, anything at all, you just ask Kayo, doll."

His casual familiarity frightened me. Did I look as if I would welcome his advances? I was in beyond my depth with Kayo. I couldn't wait to get out of there. I lay on the bed and looked up the address for the Y in the phone book, then found it on the map. It was within walking distance. I packed my bag and went downstairs.

"Leaving so soon, doll?" Kayo asked. "I'll give you one night free if you stay a week."

"I can't," I said, dropping the key on the counter.

He reached out and touched my hair. "Say, is that your real color? I never saw hair that color unless it was fake. Or on a little kid."

I pulled back from his touch and hurried out the door.

The Y wasn't in a great neighborhood, but it was better than the Edison, about the same rent, and, best of all, there was a security guard at the front door. My room may not have been much nicer than the one at the Edison, but it felt a lot safer.

I had dinner at a different coffee shop, another huge satisfying meal, eaten in air-conditioned bliss. I forced myself to think only of the food and the cool, dry air.

On the way out of the coffee shop, I passed a rack of paperback books. I spun the rack: mysteries, romances, Westerns; nothing appealed to me. They were too expensive, anyway, and I had *Jane Eyre*, unread, in my bag. Tuesday I'd find a library where I could get escape for free.

Back in my new room, I read the first two chapters of *Jane Eyre*. Poor orphaned Jane, living with a family that abused her, did nothing to cheer me up. I wished I'd brought a different book, but it was too late for that now.

After twenty pages of Jane's misery, the need for sleep made me feel drugged. I turned out the light and listened to the Saturday-night commotion in the street below. It was noisy, but not as bad as at the Hotel Edison.

All summer I'd been so tired—a kind of bone-deep exhaustion I'd thought at first was from being pregnant. Maybe that's all it really was, but I couldn't help wondering if it was compounded by how alone I felt and by how much I wanted to escape from the whole mess.

# TEN

On Sunday the buses ran on a holiday schedule, but I didn't mind waiting on benches, enjoying the sun on my face. It was nice to have an excuse to do nothing after feeling for so long that I had too much to do. After a bus ride circling the downtown area, where shops were closed and streets almost empty, I boarded a bus labeled EUSTACE PARK.

I knew from my map that Eustace Park lay on the west edge of the city. Though the bus was nearly empty when I got on, it filled up as it passed through more residential areas. Families came aboard, with picnic baskets and blankets. Children carried balls and Frisbees and stuffed animals. One little boy, the shape of whose blond head reminded me of Sonny, looked at me over the back of his seat, and when I smiled at him, he turned, wide-eyed, and sat leaning against his mother's arm.

The park was at the end of the line, and the bus emptied there. I waited so I would be the last one off. Hardly realizing what I was doing, I followed the boy and his family along the winding cement paths and stopped to watch when they spread their blanket near a small playground. The grass was dotted with other picnickers, but I stood by a larch tree, looking on as "my" little boy and his parents laid out the contents of their basket, turned on a portable radio, and the father stretched out, his head in his wife's lap.

What would it be like to grow up in such a family? I was surprised to feel a sudden spurt of anger toward the baby. For all the trouble it was causing me, it had a chance of getting the kind of family I'd always wanted and would never have.

I walked on, finding myself looking for people alone. There were a few: a man in a white shirt, asleep on his back, a newspaper over his face; a gray-haired women throwing bread to ducks in a pond; a lanky black boy roller-skating backward, his ears plugged with headphones. To my eyes, they appeared content with their solitariness. I wondered if I seemed the same to them. How could they know the terrible turmoil inside me?

As I wandered through the park, I thought again of Mama and Pop and the boys at Ambrose Lake. For the first Labor Day weekend of my life, I wasn't with them, and my memories of those weekends took on a luster they'd never had in reality. I shook my head and told myself that homesickness was one thing, but remembering a cozy, happy family to miss was something else again. Distance wasn't enough to transform Pop into Ward Cleaver, and I better not forget it.

Finally I couldn't watch those families on holiday anymore.

I took the bus back to the YWCA. I was lonely, I was being sentimental. Yet I couldn't shake the feeling that the world was full of families, sheltering and appreciating each other in a way I would never know.

Monday, I sat for a long time over breakfast, drinking too many cups of coffee, trying to decide what to do with the rest of the long empty day. Finally I paid the bill and left, just to avoid having to drink more coffee.

Disgusted with myself for my aimlessness, I decided that reading about poor Jane Eyre's plight would suit me perfectly for the rest of the day. I was on the way back to the YWCA when I passed a shop with a sign in the window: WAITRESS WANTED. INQUIRE WITHIN.

I looked up at the window and saw, in fancy gold script across the glass, the word GOURMANIAC. Below the big gold letters were smaller ones that read HOME OF THE ROUND MEAL. The window was papered from the inside, so I couldn't look in.

Impulsively, I tried the door, which, to my surprise, was unlocked. I stuck my head into a spare, bright room. Round tables of pale wood were scattered about, and a long white counter stretched across the back of the room. Healthy plants hung from the ceiling beams, and the pile of dishes and napkins on the counter were bright red.

"Anybody here?" I called.

From behind the counter rose a tall, balding man with a mustache, a potbelly, and a deep suntan. He had a screwdriver in his hand.

"Just me," he said. "Will that do?"

"I saw your sign. For the waitress."

"I just put that up. Here I am, set to open to-morrow, and the waitress I'd hired, and who completely pulled the wool over my eyes, by the way, told me last night she'd decided to go to Montana and work on a dude ranch. Can you beat that? When she could be working here instead? Are you a waitress?" he asked.

"Yes."

"Well, well. As one of my patients used to say, 'That which you are seeking is out there seeking you as well.' He was okay, once you got used to the turban."

"Your patients?"

"In my previous life, when I was a doctor. Come on in. I'll interview you." I closed the door. "Sit down over here," he said. "Best seat in the house."

I sat on the edge of a bentwood chair next to one of the round butcher-block tables. He looked harmless enough, but his talk of turbans and patients and previous lives made me nervous.

"Uh, how long ago was this previous life?" I asked.

"About a year ago. I've retired, I guess you could say."

I relaxed a little.

In the center of the table was an empty mineral-water bottle. "I'm going to put flowers in the bottles," he said. "Red ones. But not until tomorrow, opening day. That'll look nice, don't you think? How do you like these pictures, or whatever you'd call them? I saw one in the office of a doctor friend of mine, and I asked him where he got it. He gave me the name of the gallery, and I bought the last two they had."

I looked up at the pictures hanging on the wall. Collages is what they really were. All kinds of things—kitchen utensils, items of clothing, tools, toys—were piled onto the surface of the canvas, and then the whole thing had been painted white. Each collage had only one spot of color. On one, in the upper left-hand corner, was a red clothespin. On the other, right in the center, was a red tennis ball. Each picture had, inscribed across the bottom in red, the words *One Spot of Red*, followed by a number.

"They're great," I said. They really were. I stood up and looked at one of the pictures more closely. Among the items in it were a spoon, a yo-yo, a hammer, a tennis shoe, a beer bottle, a ball of twine, a ballpoint pen, and a glove. "I wonder what that clothespin means? Why is it the only red thing?"

"Doesn't necessarily mean anything," he said. "It just has to make you feel something. How does it make you feel?"

I sat down, still looking up at *One Spot of Red: No. 33*. "Interested. Curious. Kind of excited. It's so busy, but the white evens it all out, except for the red spot. Why is the clothespin more special than the beer bottle or the tennis shoe?"

"I don't know. But I bet the artist does. Scarlet is the color of passion."

I didn't know what to say to that. This was the first time I'd ever discussed art with anyone; maybe the word *passion* was common in art talk, but it made me uncomfortable. "Why is this the 'home of the round meal'?" I asked, to change the subject. "You've heard of square meals. Well, I serve round ones. After all, plates are round. I'm going to serve only round food. Almost all breakfast food is round. Did you ever think about that? Pancakes and bagels, fried eggs and English muffins. Doughnuts and sausage patties. Grapefruit and bowls of cereal. I know, that's sort of cheating. It's the bowl, not the cereal, that's round. But it works out okay. Lots of lunch food is round, too. Hamburgers and pizza. Pita sandwiches. Slices of salami and tomato. Pickle chips. Potato chips. Pies. Cupcakes. Bowls of soup. You can shape almost anything into a round. So it's a gimmick. Everybody needs a gimmick. I'm only going to be open for breakfast and lunch, Monday through Saturday. There's no dinner business around here, anyway. Nobody hangs around after five or six o'clock. They all take off for the suburbs. Breakfast and lunch, that's what I do best. Anyway, it's hard to find round dinner food. You ever hear of a round chicken? There *is* round steak, I guess, but there's not enough other variety. So, what do you think?"

"I noticed the tables are round."

"Good. You pass the interview. You're hired. Can you start tomorrow morning at six-thirty? I'll pay you minimum wage plus tips and meals. What's your name?"

"Daphne Blake. What's yours?"

"T. Peter Perry. Ex-M.D. Ex-husband. Ex-member of the rat race. Soon to be restaurateur, philosopher, human being." He smiled expansively, and I couldn't help smiling back.

"What should I wear, Mr. Perry?"

"Call me T. Peter. And you'll wear this." He went behind the counter and returned with a red apron and a red T-shirt with GOURMANIAC in white script across the front. "See you at six-thirty. Oh," he added, handing me an employment application, "fill this out and bring it with you in the morning."

He took my elbow and propelled me out the door, closing it behind me. I stood on the sidewalk, the apron and T-shirt in my hand, feeling about the way I had when I looked at *One Spot of Red: No. 33*—interested, curious, and very excited. Without even trying, I had a job! In a pretty place, with a nice boss! The shadow of fear and doubt that had pressed so closely against me since I left Seeley seemed to recede a little.

Sleeping, reading, filling out my application, and doing hand laundry took up the rest of the afternoon. At dinnertime, I ate at the same coffee shop where I'd had breakfast. I noticed that, without thinking, I'd ordered a round meal: soup with oyster crackers, and a hamburger.

As I slid into bed that night, I realized that what I had done was now irrevocable. Mama and Pop were home, had read my note, and knew I was gone. I wondered how hard it had been for Mama to act surprised.

I lay in the dark, feeling that tiny, fragile link with her, and wiped my tears on the pillowcase.

# ELEVEN

For all my good intentions, I hardly slept that night. My room was hot, the street noises were loud, and I was too full of too many conflicting emotions: relief, fear, regret, shame, anger, envy, resentment. My hormones were fluctuating, my mind wouldn't get out of overdrive, and I had to keep getting up to go to the bathroom. I was relieved when daylight came and I could quit trying to sleep. There was plenty of time before I was due at work, but I needed to escape from my busy mind.

I decided to leave early and help T. Peter open the Gourmaniac. As I pulled on my T-shirt, I wondered how much longer it would fit. The waistband of my jeans was already too tight.

At six o'clock I rapped on the door of the Gourmaniac, and T. Peter, in a T-shirt which matched mine and with a knife in his hand, opened the door.

"Can you start setting tables?" he asked. "The silver's behind the counter. I'm slicing oranges, and Junior Lee's making sausage patties."

"Sure. Who's Junior Lee?" I tied on my apron.

"Junior Lee!" T. Peter bellowed.

A tall, skinny boy who looked about eighteen and was the color of bittersweet chocolate popped out of the kitchen. "Yo!" he said, wiping his hands on his Gourmaniac apron.

"Junior Lee, this is Daphne. She's our waitress. Daphne, this is Junior Lee, our cook."

"Hi, Daffy. How did you get a name like that?" He popped back into the kitchen without waiting for an answer. "Work to do," he called.

For the next thirty minutes, T. Peter, Junior Lee, and I were in a whirl of activity, readying the Gourmaniac for its first round meal.

"I didn't sleep a wink last night," T. Peter said, mixing pancake batter. "I'm nervous as a rutabaga."

"I've never heard that expression before," I said.

"Neither have I," T. Peter said. "It doesn't make sense, does it? Just shows you how nervous I am. What if nobody comes? What if I've spent all this money and effort and longing and desire, and nobody's interested? I can't be responsible for my actions if that happens. I'll . . ."

"Zounds, chief," Junior Lee said, standing in the kitchen doorway. "Look out the window. Appears to be customers. Better open the door."

T. Peter went to the door, saying over his shoulder, "Probably none of them wanted breakfast. They're just looking for directions, or a place to go to the bathroom."

Either everybody downtown showed up out of curiosity on the first day any new restaurant opened or the Gourmaniac *was* just what they had all been waiting for. Customers poured into the tiny shop, and there was a line on the sidewalk: men in business suits, their jackets over their arms, fanning themselves with newspapers; women in summer dresses and high-heeled sandals; T-shirted messenger boys.

It was pandemonium. I couldn't remember where anything was, and I didn't know what anything cost because I hadn't even seen a menu and didn't have time to look.

The customers didn't seem to mind the confusion. They were fresh from a three-day weekend, and still in a holiday mood. When T. Peter, Junior Lee, and I all collided in the kitchen doorway, the people at the counter applauded and laughed. We giggled a little hysterically as we disentangled ourselves, but we had caught the party spirit, too. It was nothing at all like working at Charlie's.

About ten o'clock the crowd began to thin, then picked up again around eleven, with people coming in for coffee breaks, and built to a crescendo at lunch, once more with people spilling out onto the sidewalk.

At twelve-thirty, T. Peter stood on a just-vacated stool at the counter, the only empty seat in the place, and announced, "Can I have your attention?"

Startled customers looked up and stopped talking. I turned off the milk-shake machine.

"I just want to thank you all for coming today," he said. "Having this place is my lifelong dream, but I couldn't do it without you. There's a free cookie for everybody who comes up and shakes my hand before he or she leaves."

Junior Lee stepped out of the kitchen and grabbed

T. Peter's hand. "Where's my cookie, man? I'm leaving."

I figured he was kidding, but I wasn't sure until T. Peter said, "No cookie for you—ever," and gave him a push back into the kitchen. "You're indispensable."

At two-thirty T. Peter locked the front door and hung up the CLOSED sign, and the three of us sagged onto stools in front of the counter, waiting for the last two tables of lunchers to finish eating and leave.

"God, wasn't it great?" T. Peter said. "All those people."

"You think we're gonna have to do this again tomorrow?" Junior Lee asked.

"Of course we are. I can hardly wait. Can you?"

"Well, I hope I heal up by then." He stuck his arms out in front of him, showing undersides marked with burns. "This here's from a fried egg," he said, pointing, "and this one's from a hamburger, and this one—"

"Ye gads!" T. Peter yelped, jumping to his feet. "Why didn't you say something? I'll be right back." He ran through the kitchen, and we could hear him thumping up stairs.

"Where's he going?" I asked.

"He lives in the apartment up there."

Junior Lee got up to take money and open the door for the last customers.

T. Peter pounded down the stairs and ran to Junior Lee, extending a tube of burn cream. "Here. I can't have my colleagues disabled. I need you."

Junior Lee took the tube and began spreading ointment on his arms. "How come I'm doing this myself? I thought you were a doctor. How come I'm not hooked up to some tubes with a pretty nurse holding my hand, like in the movies?"

"I'm retired, Junior Lee. You're on your own. But I think I can safely say you'll survive. Now let's eat. I'm starved."

"You're welcome to whatever you can find lying around in there," Junior Lee said, "but I'm through cooking for today. Anyway, I'm *hors de combat*."

"*Hors de combat*, are you?" T. Peter asked. "Fortunately I know that's French for out of action. You trying to impress me?"

"What do you think I'm going to City College for, anyway? What good's education if you can't hit people over the head with it now and then? Cooking's just entertainment for me. I'm a serious student."

"Well, I know how to do some serious cooking. Go sit at a table and lay some of that education on Daphne, while I rustle up our lunch." He headed for the kitchen.

Junior Lee and I moved to a clean table, where he stretched out his arms and blew on the burns. "You're a stepper, Daffy," he said to me. "I like working with somebody like that."

"Thanks. My name's Daphne."

"Well, Daffy suits you better. All those yellow curls. Okay if I call you that?"

"Sure." I'd never had a nickname before. The closest I'd come to one was when Scott called me Daf. As silly as it sounded, I liked having Junior Lee name me Daffy.

"Yeah," Junior Lee went on. "You know how to hustle. I've worked with some natural born simpletons who don't do thing one without written directions from God Almighty and delivered in person."

I laughed. He talked with an energy I'd never heard before, and it made everything he said sound exciting. "I mean to tell you, I have worked with some world-class losers. If loafing was an Olympic event, these guys would be gold-medal winners. And then, and *then*"—his voice rose half an octave— "they're the first ones to complain about how hard they're working. It's enough to make a reasonable man violent." He blew on his arms again. "That's why I decided to go to college, no matter what it took. I'm not spending the rest of my life working with doofs like that. I want to work with doofs in three-piece suits."

"How can you go to college and work here?" I asked.

"I go to college at night. City College. Work days. Study in the afternoons or late at night. Cut up any time in between."

"Sounds hard."

"Hard? That might sound hard to any ordinary mortal, but for Junior Lee Jenkins, it's nothing. The merest backbreaking struggle. I do rejoice in an impossible challenge."

T. Peter arrived with three plates of hamburgers and potato rounds, and plunked them on the table. "Eat, my friends," he commanded, dropping into a chair between me and Junior Lee.

"You *can* cook," Junior Lee said, his mouth full. "A man of many talents."

"Like you, Junior Lee, like you," T. Peter answered.

"Come on, you weren't really a doctor, were you?" Junior Lee asked. "Anybody can have a tube of burn medicine."

"Indeed, I was. Twenty-two years a surgeon. A good one, too. There wasn't a bowel I couldn't unobstruct, a gallbladder I couldn't . . ."

"I get the idea, chief. We're eating, remember?"

"Sorry."

"So why did you quit?" I asked.

"I got tired of it. You can't do that when you're a doctor. You have to stay fascinated by seeing patients. I wanted to concentrate more on people's outsides than their insides, and I'd always wanted to open a restaurant. Contrary to the impression given you by my youthful appearance"—he smoothed his hand over his balding head—"I'm not a kid anymore. I figured I'd better get with it. Unfortunately, my wife wasn't enthusiastic about the idea, so now she's my ex-wife. She got most of the money—that was her favorite part of me, anyway, I always thought—but I had enough left for the Gourmaniac, and that's all I wanted."

"Do you have children?" I asked. T. Peter seemed as exotic to me as Junior Lee. I couldn't imagine giving up a career as a surgeon to open a restaurant like the Gourmaniac.

"Two boys. They're both in college, and I'm sorry to say I don't know them very well. I wasn't around much when they were growing up. I took my responsibilities as provider very seriously, but I missed out on knowing the family I was providing for. I bet an educated man like Junior Lee knows what to call that."

"Right on," Junior Lee said. "First I call it irony. Then I call it too bad." His voice was serious.

"That's what I call it, too," T. Peter said. "Well, that's enough true confessions from the boss. Why don't you kids go out and buy some records or dye your hair green or whatever kids do today? I'll clean up."

"It's a deal, chief," Junior Lee said, standing up. "Classes start tonight, and I want to fritter away my last few carefree hours before I put my shoulder to the wheel, my neck in the harness, and my nose to the grindstone. See you two tomorrow, bright and early." As he went out the door, he called back, "Hey, can I get worker's comp for these here injuries?" T. Peter just laughed, and Junior Lee left.

I should have left, too, but it felt so good to be in this bright happy place, I didn't want to go.

"Come on," I said to T. Peter. "I'll help you clean up."

"Oh, you go on home. I can do it."

"I want to help. If you're as tired as I am, you shouldn't turn me down."

"I am tired. What a wild day."

"Tomorrow's bound to be easier. None of us knew what we were doing." I began gathering up the dirty dishes.

"But it was still fun, wasn't it?"

I considered that. "You're right. It was fun."

"I'm glad you thought so. Attitude's important in this business."

"Probably in any business."

"Right you are. I must have been very good in a previous incarnation to deserve you and Junior Lee. Noreen's better off on the dude ranch."

# TWELVE

A ll my energy seemed to have been left at the Gourmaniac. I was so tired I could hardly walk the few blocks to the YWCA. But it was a good, physical tiredness that came from working hard—not the stressed, tight exhaustion I'd been feeling all summer. I plodded blindly through the lobby and went straight upstairs to bed.

Before I knew it, it was time to get up and go to work again. This time, I went in early enough to have an orange, an egg, and an English muffin before the doors opened. For the baby.

The Gourmaniac was as busy as it had been the day before, and T. Peter was as manic. He passed out pink bubble-gum cigars, with bands on them reading IT'S A RESTAURANT, to all the customers, and his laughter punctuated the clatter and conversation. After the CLOSED sign had been hung in the window, he again made me and Junior Lee sit at a table while he fixed lunch for the three of us.

"What did you learn at college last night, Junior Lee?" I asked. If I were still at home, I'd have begun my senior year the day before. Now I wasn't sure if I'd ever be in school again. It gave me hope to know that Junior Lee was in college, even though he thought it was merely a backbreaking struggle.

"Well, let's see. I learned how to sleep with my eyes open. And how to get the good-looking girl next to me to take notes for me—all these burns, you know, they make it hard—and I learned a couple of nonessential facts about history or math or whatever class that was." He took a long drink of his lemonade.

"I thought you were a serious student."

"Oh, I'm serious. But just when I'm studying. You ever notice how dead-grim real life is unless you make a violent effort to the contrary?"

"Sure. But not everybody can make those violent efforts to the contrary." I hoped I was still one who could.

"Well, you got to try. Otherwise, that bugger'll just chew you up and spit you out."

T. Peter put a plate piled with cheese-and-bacon hotcakes on the table. "Luncheon is served."

We dived in.

"You go to school, Daffy?" Junior Lee asked.

"No. No, not right now . . ."

"Well, maybe later. Or maybe you've had enough."

"No, I haven't had enough. It's just . . . it's not the right time for school now. I have . . . something else to do."

"Right," Junior Lee said.

"What about you?" I asked. "What are you going to do when you finish school?" It was safer to keep the conversation off me.

"I'm not one hundred percent sure yet, but I know I want to have my own business. Like my idol here, Mr. T. Peter Perry. I'm going to be an entrepreneur. Build an empire. Become a tycoon. I just got to find my spot."

"I have no doubt that you can do it, Junior Lee," T. Peter said. "It was a lucky day for me when you came through that door looking for a job. If I had even half your energy, they'd have to keep me in a cage."

"Aw, shucks," Junior Lee said, hiding his face in his hands. "I'd be embarrassed if it wasn't true." He looked up. "It's my personal theory that there is no such thing as too much praise. I was raised by my Aunt Clementine, and that woman knew how to praise! She praised the Lord, praised the government, praised the gas and electric company, praised everybody she knew, and there were three hundred people at her funeral. I decided that if everybody raised kids by ignoring what they did wrong and praising what they did right, there wouldn't be any bad kids. I don't think there's any chance of my theory getting tested, but I bet it would work."

It sounded wonderful to me. I wondered how I would have turned out if I'd been raised that way. Maybe I wouldn't have been so vulnerable to Scott, so eager to please, so afraid of scaring him away. But he left anyway, didn't he?

Junior Lee dabbed his lips with a napkin. "Well, fans, I got to jam. Places to go and people to see.

Until mañana. Did you hear that? Another language to dazzle you with." He went out the door, whistling.

T. Peter began gathering up plates. "Why don't you take off, too, Daphne? You must have things to do."

"Nothing that won't wait. I like to stay and help you." The last thing I wanted to do was return to the solitude of the YWCA.

"You don't have to twist my arm. I welcome the company. I spent almost the whole summer alone and got my maximum daily allowance of solitude for a while."

"What did you do?" I collected the rest of the dishes and carried them to the kitchen.

"I floated around on a sailboat in the Caribbean for two months. Friend of mine was spending the summer in Europe, and he let me use his boat. I didn't go anywhere in it—just floated, fished, swam, put in for supplies once in a while, anchored every night. I never got out of sight of land. I needed to spend some time with myself. It was great at first, but it's like when you're thirsty: you feel like you'll die if you can't have a drink—that you'll kill anybody who gets between you and water. Then, when you've drunk so much you feel like your stomach's going to rupture, you're ready to kill the next person who offers you a drink. Timing is everything."

"I guess that's true," I said, thinking that my timing was way off with regard to school, motherhood, and everything else I could think of.

# THIRTEEN

E very morning of that first week, T. Peter was
as excited as he had been on opening day. His
delight in his new business was contagious; Junior
Lee and I and even the customers caught it. He
greeted people at the door as if they were visiting
relatives, and made them promise to come back
before he let them pay their checks. He gave a free
dessert to anyone marking a special occasion that
day, and it didn't have to be a birthday or an an-
niversary. People with dentist appointments got
free dessert, and so did those who had bought a new
dress or gotten a haircut.

Nothing fazed Junior Lee. He cooked special orders without grumbling, came out of the kitchen to
see how the customers liked his food, and redid
anything that anyone complained about, though
there were few complaints.

He and T. Peter were either praising each other
extravagantly as "the finest restaurateur in the history of the universe" and "the most imaginative

cook east of the Pyrenees," or insulting each other equally extravagantly. T. Peter was "the most heartless slave driver in Western Christendom," and Junior Lee's food was "so ill prepared he's wanted in six states for disturbing the digestion." They praised me, too, as "the most fulgent flower of femininity" and "the only light in our miserable lives," but they saved their insults for each other. Such courtliness gave me a feeling of being treasured that I'd never had before.

That first Sunday, when the Gourmaniac was closed, I was finally able to sleep later than sunrise. Even so, the day ahead of me was long and passed slowly. I missed the bustle of the Gourmaniac, the pleasure of working with T. Peter and Junior Lee, and our leisurely lunches after closing: all the things that occupied me, entertained me, and kept me from thinking of home, and why I wasn't there.

All during that day I thought, Mama will be home from church by now, or Sonny'll be going down for his nap about this time. I wondered how the older boys had liked their first week of school, and how Mama was getting along without my help. I hoped Pop hadn't taken out his anger at my leaving on her or the boys.

I took a long walk, read *Jane Eyre*, and told myself to stop thinking about what was happening at home. That had nothing to do with me anymore. Still, by evening, I felt sad and lonely and fearful. My isolation was too oppressive. I was ready to be at the Gourmaniac again. It was a secure place in the mess of my life.

\* \* \*

At noon on Monday, I had just delivered a deluxe hamburger to a man in a bright blue suit sitting at the counter, and was reaching for the coffeepot, when I felt a tug on my apron string. I turned, grabbing my slipping apron, to find the blue-suited man standing, leaning over the counter, his face red.

"Hey, honey, I'm not paying for this."

"Is there something wrong?"

"I'll say there's something wrong. I don't call a lettuce-and-tomato sandwich a hamburger. What are you trying to pull here?"

T. Peter appeared behind the man and pressed him back onto the stool with a hand on his shoulder. "Having a problem, sir?" he asked.

"Yeah. I got a problem. There's no meat on this bun."

"Yes? I congratulate you on your health-consciousness, sir," T. Peter said smoothly. "Most of us eat far too much red meat."

"I *ordered* a hamburger," the red-faced man said.

"Oh. In that case, I congratulate you on your discernment. We serve the finest beef in town." He picked up the plate. "I'll just step into the kitchen and make sure you get it while I fire the cook. No problem. Daphne, give the gentleman a free lemonade while I take care of this."

I wanted to pour the lemonade in his lap, but I set it in front of him and went into the kitchen.

"Throw a hamburger on this bun, Junior Lee," T. Peter was saying, "and I'll restrain myself from spitting on it."

"What's up?" Junior Lee asked, flipping burgers.

"Some jerk wanting to make a scene over an honest mistake. You forgot the meat on his sandwich."

"My, my," Junior Lee said. "A professional jackass."

"I see you know the type."

Junior Lee slipped a burger onto the bun, and the three of us looked down at it. T. Peter cleared his throat. Junior Lee did, too, and they both looked at me. When I followed suit, we all laughed.

"We can pretend we did," T. Peter said, and took the plate back to the man, who ate and departed without leaving a tip.

After closing, as T. Peter carried a pizza in from the kitchen, I brought the incident up. "I wanted to punch him in the nose. Some people go out of their way to make things hard." Pop's face swam through my mind.

"Too true," T. Peter said. "But I want this to be a happy place. That's my job. I'd just as soon not see *him* again, though."

"Well, you were so nice, he probably *will* come back."

"Why, Daffy, don't tell me you're surprised at how charming our chief can be," Junior Lee said, going from table to table, wiping up crumbs and spills.

"For heaven's sake," T. Peter said, "can't you sit still? You wear me out watching you. Come eat. At least you have to sit down to do that."

Junior Lee settled into his chair and took a piece of pizza from the tray, dragging strings of melted cheese across the table.

"Gracious dining," T. Peter said, shaking his head.

"Now, what's the important part here?" Junior Lee asked. "The fact that we're chewing food to-

gether, or the fact that we're spending time together, getting to know each other, getting used to
each other? In a little operation like this, man,
teamwork's a very important thing. The more con-
genial we are, the better we'll work together and
the better it'll be for business. See? So the chewing's
secondary. Give me another piece of pizza."

"You're not acting like it's secondary," T. Peter
said.

"I'm a growing boy, chief. I've got to keep up my
strength."

"Well, leave some for Daphne. She's got some
strength to keep up, too."

Junior Lee turned to me. "You know, Daffy, you
look a mite peaky. You okay?"

Had they guessed something about me? Why
would T. Peter say I needed to keep up my strength?
Just because I was working hard, or did he know
about the baby? He was a doctor, after all. And what
did Junior Lee mean by "peaky"? Pregnant?

"I'm fine," I said quickly. "Just a little tired.
Where I worked before we were hardly ever this
busy. I guess because the food was so bad."

"Here in Lincoln?" T. Peter asked.

"No. It was . . . a little town southwest of here."

"You been here long?" Junior Lee asked.

"Not too long. How about you?" I didn't want to
talk about myself.

"Born and raised here. Learned all my street
smarts not too far from this very spot. Probably be
here forever, too. It feels like home. How about you,
chief?"

"I lived in the suburbs—Cedar Heights—for
twenty years. All I'd do is drive from my house to

my office in Lincoln. Hardly knew what downtown looked like. Just shuttled between my pockets of illusion."

"Don't knock it," Junior Lee said. "There's a lot to be said for illusion. There's plenty of the real thing you wouldn't actually want to look too hard at."

"That's so. And I suppose we create our own illusions—the ones we need."

"Ain't that right, chief. We all need our clouds of laughing gas to walk around in."

"I don't want to be alone in my cloud," T. Peter said. "I want lots of company. That's one reason for the Gourmaniac. I want my customers to be more than that—I want them to be like family. I want people to bring their children in here and tell them this is where they courted. I want to have Christmas parties and—"

"That's all fine, chief, just as long as you don't start giving away too many free meals. Then you'll be out there with the street people your own self."

"But by then, Junior Lee, you'll be a tycoon and you'll give me a job, won't you? Your old idol, T. Peter, could work for you."

Junior Lee threw back his head and laughed. "What about Daffy? We'll have to find something for her to do, too. We don't want her out wandering around by herself."

It felt to me as if I'd spent most of my life wandering around by myself. Sometimes I'd bumped into other people as I wandered—Susan, Mama, Sonny, even Scott—but I'd never felt that some other person had linked arms with me and walked in step. Depending on someone else was a dangerous idea, and, like many other dangerous ideas, it had its attractions. Since Scott, they were attractions I was more determined than ever to resist.

"Well, I know one thing," Junior Lee said, standing up. "We'll all be right here tomorrow morning, so let's not worry yet. I got to go do some tearing up now, so I'll see you folks later." He patted me on the head, and boogied to the door.

I could hardly wait to hear what Junior Lee would have to say the next day. In the short time I'd known him, I'd been amazed at the number of subjects he had opinions on. He thought windows should be washed counterclockwise; the government should print more money so everybody would have enough; parking meters should take dollar bills for all-day parking; making beds was a waste of time; everybody should do twenty push-ups a day for upper-body strength.

At lunch, after listening to Junior Lee carry on for half an hour, T. Peter had once said, "You're going to burn yourself up if you're not careful, Junior Lee. You need somebody to put a leash on you."

"I'm hard to tame, that's the truth. My Aunt Clementine did a pretty good job of it, but since she's been gone, I'm getting wild again. There's some kind of motor in me that won't stop running."

"It needs channeling," T. Peter said. "You can be head of a million-dollar corporation or an evil genius."

"Those my only two choices? I bet I could do them both at the same time with one hand tied behind me."

T. Peter laughed. "I believe you."

# FOURTEEN

The end of September came and I still hadn't made an appointment at a clinic. I banked my paycheck and half my tips, keeping the rest for what Junior Lee called "walking-around money," though I didn't do much walking around. I didn't do much anything.

Even as I felt my center of gravity change, and the baby become more of a reality, I tried to ignore what was happening. The more of my body the baby took over, the less of my mind I gave up to it. I took care of my everyday business and acted as if there wouldn't be a tomorrow. It was as though, by not planning for the future, I could prevent it—and the baby—from coming.

On the first day of October, I arrived at work to find T. Peter nailing a mug rack to the wall by the cash register.

"What's that for?"

"We've got enough regulars now to have some

mugs for them. I've always wanted to do that, and I can't wait any longer."

"So who gets a mug?" Junior Lee asked over the pass-through to the kitchen.

T. Peter reached under the counter and pulled out a red mug with Junior Lee's name on it in white. "First, you do. Then"—he pulled out another mug with my name on it—"Daphne, and then me. There's nobody more regular than us."

I held the mug in my two hands and was mortified to find tears misting my eyes. I'd never received a gift so personal and so intimate, and I was tempted to give it back, saying I didn't deserve it, and I didn't want the expectations that went with it. Instead, I said nothing. Neither did Junior Lee.

"Gee," T. Peter said in a downcast voice. "I was hoping for more enthusiasm. Can't you humor me a little?"

Junior Lee cleared his throat. "You just learned my secret, chief. Strong emotion's about the only thing that shuts me up."

"Me, too," I told him, feeling sure I didn't mean it the same way Junior Lee did.

"That's better," T. Peter said. "Shall we christen them?" He poured coffee for us all, and we toasted each other.

"So who else is lucky enough to get one of these babies?" Junior Lee asked, blowing on his coffee.

T. Peter lined up several mugs on the counter. Each had a white name printed on it. "There's one for Mr. Sedgewick, the bank president. You know, orange juice, corned beef hash, and poached egg at eight every morning. One for Paddy Riordan, plaid suit, doughnuts at ten o'clock."

"That suit belongs under a saddle," Junior Lee said, "but Paddy, he's okay."

"One for Laura and one for Annie, the secretaries, milk and cookies at two. One for Mattie, gray hair, overalls, soup at eleven-thirty."

"The lady with the motorbike?" Junior Lee asked.

"That's the one."

I knew who they all were. They seemed to have a luster that the regulars at Charlie's never had. Or maybe it was T. Peter's luster that spread over the Gourmaniac's regulars. "Won't they be surprised," I said, for lack of anything else to say.

They were, and T. Peter was so pleased by their response that he laughed out loud and came into the kitchen to clink his mug against mine and Junior Lee's one more time.

"You know, Daffy," Junior Lee said after closing that day, as we waited for T. Peter to finish preparing our lunch. "I don't ever hear you talking about your family."

"You don't much, either. Neither does T. Peter."

"Must mean we feel real private about them."

"Or they're something we don't like to talk about," I said.

"Or they're nonexistent," T. Peter said, lounging by the kitchen door.

"Don't you ever see your boys?" I asked.

"Not a lot. They're away at school, and when we do see each other we don't know what to say or where to start. Someday maybe we'll get to know one another. But then again, we might not. They've gotten along so far, mostly without me. Why should they suddenly change?"

"Maybe they've always missed having a dad," I suggested.

T. Peter shrugged. "No signs of that so far."

"I've always missed having a dad," I said, "and I have one." Why had I said that? It wasn't the kind of thing I told anybody.

"The same way my kids had one? Gone all the time?"

"No. I just didn't get along with him." That seemed the least I could say without being rude.

"Well, I must have had a dad," Junior Lee said, "or else I'm some kind of miracle, but he split before I showed up. Then my mother took off, too. All I've got is a couple of pictures of them."

We sat in silence for a moment, and then Junior Lee said, "We ever gonna get any lunch?"

T. Peter went into the kitchen and came back carrying a tray. "I have a surprise. It's quiche." He put a small quiche pan in front of each of us. "Tell me if you think it's good enough to add to the menu."

I poked a few holes in my quiche to cool it. "Running a restaurant seems like a logical thing for an ex-doctor to do."

"What makes you think so?" T. Peter asked.

"You're still taking care of people the way you run the Gourmaniac—like a party."

"You know what was the worst thing about being a doctor?" he asked.

"People not paying their bills on time," Junior Lee said, his mouth full of quiche. "Coughing up so much to the IRS. This stuff is *good*, chief. You'll have to show me how to make it."

"I will. No, the worst thing was when somebody

died, after I'd done everything I could think of to keep them alive. One day I decided I couldn't stand to have that happen again, and that's when I retired."

"Well, I haven't killed anybody yet with my cooking," Junior Lee said.

"Oh, stop, Junior Lee," I said, touched by the sorrow I'd heard in T. Peter's voice. "Dying people aren't funny." Was it my fluctuating hormones? I couldn't remember ever scolding anyone but my brothers, and then only rarely. Now, here I was chastising Junior Lee for making a harmless joke.

"Don't pay no attention to me, Daffy. It's just my way."

"I'm sorry," I said, contrite. "I know it is. I don't know why I said that."

"Children, children," T. Peter interjected. "It's all right. I shouldn't have started it. It's not your concern."

He was right, it wasn't my concern. I didn't want it to be my concern. And yet I was moved by T. Peter's sorrow and compassion. I took refuge in a swallow of coffee.

"Daffy's right," Junior Lee said. "I just can't help acting like a fool sometimes. But we got to tend to each other. If we don't, who's going to?"

"I like the way you think, Junior Lee," T. Peter said. "And everybody's entitled to act like a fool once in a while."

"Well, you let me know when I'm overdoing it. I don't want to use up my quota."

"I think you can count on Daphne to do that," T. Peter said, laughing.

"Oh, no," I said. "I shouldn't have said anything."

"Daphne," T. Peter said, patting my arm. "You didn't do a thing wrong. It's all right to speak your mind. How else are we going to get to know what's in it?"

I wasn't sure *I* knew what was in it. And the parts I was sure about weren't things I wanted to tell anybody else.

When I didn't reply, T. Peter said, "Any time you're ready, we'll be listening. It's okay."

"Sure it is, Daffy. Just next time you give me any lip, I'll bust out crying." Junior Lee looked at my face and said, "I'm kidding, I'm kidding. Guess I used up some more of my fool allowance, huh?"

"We'll let you know, Junior Lee," T. Peter said. "After all, what are friends for?"

# FIFTEEN

I t rained almost every day in October, and the customers came into the Gourmaniac dripping and grumbling. T. Peter and Junior Lee made it their job to cheer up everybody who walked through the door. Junior Lee started wearing a pair of glasses with an attached nose and mustache, and he served each meal with a prize: a balloon, a fortune cookie, a little plastic animal.

T. Peter went around wearing a pair of glasses with eyeballs dangling from springs. Those bloodshot, bouncing eyeballs were so gross you had to laugh.

I laughed more in those days than I had since the early months of going with Scott. The way T. Peter and Junior Lee carried on, it was impossible not to.

It was Sunday that was still hard. That's the day I couldn't pretend anymore. I had to remember that I really was pregnant, that no matter what else ever happened to me, my life was forever marked by that fact. Yet I still hadn't gotten to a clinic, and I had no plan for what I would do after I gave the baby up.

On Sunday, I didn't laugh. On Sunday, I was frightened and sad and angry at Scott and at the baby for doing this to me. On Sunday, I was alone and overwhelmed and deprived of my future, my present, even my past. The baby had begun to move inside me, and the sensation was so strange I even felt deprived of my own body.

On Sunday, I thought of home. I wondered if Mama was okay, if the boys missed me, and how angry Pop was.

I understood better now how Mama's fear of Pop immobilized her. My own complicated emotions, which definitely included fear, were doing the same thing to me.

The desire to know how Mama was grew until one Monday, after work, I couldn't resist. Pop would be at work: I could call Mama and tell her she didn't have to worry about me.

I sat in the phone booth in the lobby of the Y, listening to the faraway ringing. Through the glass door I could see the security guard standing on the front steps. The phone rang and rang, and I was about to hang up when Mama, breathless, answered.

"Mama, it's Daphne. Can you talk?"

There was a silence in which I could hear her breathing, jerky and fast, as if she were crying.

"Mama? I'm okay. What's wrong?"

"When you didn't call, I thought I'd never hear from you again," she whispered.

"Oh, Mama, how could you think that?"

"Where are you?"

"I'd better not tell you. But I'm fine. I have a good job and enough money. How are the boys?"

"They've all got the chicken pox. For two weeks, all I've done is give baking soda baths and try to keep them from scratching. Even that wouldn't be so bad if your father didn't have it, too. He's the worst—"

"You mean he's home? Now?"

"He hasn't worked in a week, and he's like a caged tiger."

"Oh, Mama, I'd better hang up. If he knew you were talking to me, he'd—"

"You're damn right he would." Pop's voice cut across mine. He'd either picked up the bedroom extension or grabbed the phone from Mama. "What have you got to say for yourself, girl?" he thundered. "You didn't fool me with that note about needing to live your own life. You got yourself into some kind of trouble, didn't you? And I bet I know what it is."

"I'm not coming home, Pop. I'm fine here." I wasn't going to let him bully me long-distance.

"It's a good thing you're not coming back because if you try it you'll find the door locked against you. Nobody runs away from my house, especially knocked up, and then comes back begging. Once you're gone, you're gone."

"Don't worry. I won't be back. I'll never again live in a house where everybody's afraid all the time. You've taught me everything about what I don't want." The thunder of my heart was so loud I could hardly hear myself.

"Shut up. What do you know about anything?

You can't blame me for what you've done yourself. It's not my fault you got yourself in trouble."

There was no point in trying to explain anything to Pop. He saw life one way—*his* way—and never relented. And his way would never be my way.

"Bye, Mama," I said, in case she was still on the line. "Kiss the boys for me." The dial tone buzzed in my ear.

I hung up the receiver and rested my forehead against the phone-booth wall. I couldn't let myself cry. I wasn't going to walk through the lobby crying.

Finally I opened the folding door and stepped out. My footsteps rang on the dingy tile floor, making a forlorn and hollow sound. I ran for the stairs. It seemed impossible and ridiculous that I could miss a home that had Pop in it, but Mama and the boys were there, too, and miss it I did.

The next morning, it was still raining hard enough to affect business at the Gourmaniac. The regulars had been in, all of them complaining about the weather, but almost no one else. At eleven-thirty only one table was occupied, and that by a regular: Mattie, the lady in overalls with the motorbike. Her long, yellow slicker was slung over the back of her chair, and she looked wet and cross.

I had just put a bowl of vegetable soup and a cup of tea down on her table when the room seemed to tilt around me. The next thing I knew, I was lying on the floor next to Mattie's table. Mattie, T. Peter with his dangling eyeballs, and Junior Lee with his plastic mustache all looked down at me. I tried to smile reassuringly at them and found that I couldn't accomplish even that simple act.

"Daphne!" T. Peter said, kneeling beside me. "What happened?"

"I guess I fainted."

"I'm taking you upstairs. You can lie down on my couch until you feel better."

"But the lunchtime customers . . ."

"Don't worry about it. I doubt we'll be very busy, anyway. Junior Lee and I can handle it. You know how he feels about impossible challenges." He put his arms under mine and levered me up. I had another whirling feeling once I was on my feet, but I closed my eyes and it dissipated. T. Peter kept a tight grip on me.

"I could sit with her," Mattie offered. "I don't think she should be left alone."

"That's a good idea," T. Peter said. "It's probably only her little drinking problem. She just needs to sleep it off." He smiled at me, but he looked worried.

He and Mattie helped me up the stairs to his apartment, where they put me on the couch in the tiny living room and covered me with a blanket. T. Peter took my pulse, then went to his bedroom for a stethoscope and a blood-pressure cuff. After he'd used both on me, he stroked my hair and said, "Everything seems okay. Just get some rest."

Mattie pulled a chair closer to the couch and sat in it, saying, "Don't you worry. I'll watch her." T. Peter nodded and went downstairs again.

I closed my eyes. Every time I opened them, I got the swirling feeling, so I quit trying. After a while I dozed, and when I woke up, my head felt clearer. When I tried to sit up, Mattie moved to help me.

"Feeling better?" she asked.

"Yes. Thank you. I don't know what happened."

"Maybe you're overdoing it a little."

"Waitressing's not that hard."

"But it might be too much for somebody your age in your condition."

I looked at her. "My condition?"

"You can't fool me, kid," Mattie said. "How far along are you?"

I'd been wondering how long it would be before someone noticed. By denying the reality myself, I'd hoped to hide it from anybody else, even when I knew that was impossible. "How could you tell?" I asked softly.

"I'm no dummy. I've been around the block a few times. Your problem's not one that stays hidden very well, either. When is this little one due?"

There was no use pretending. She knew. Finally I said, "End of February, beginning of March."

Mattie was quiet for a moment, calculating. "So you're about five months along. You married?"

I looked at my hands in my lap and shook my head.

"Live with your folks?"

I shook my head again.

"With the father?"

"No."

"You're handling this all by yourself?" Mattie asked. "How old are you?"

"Seventeen."

"Oh, child. What a job. Have you been to a doctor?"

"No, not yet. I've been meaning to, but I just haven't gotten around to it. But I have some books about being pregnant from the library, and I've been taking extra-strength vitamins." I looked at

Mattie. "And I don't smoke or drink, and I get lots of sleep and drink a quart of milk every day." I wanted her to know I wasn't some irresponsible kid, even though that's how I was feeling.

"Well, you're a good, capable girl, but you still shouldn't be fainting. I'd say you need a thorough examination."

"I'll go this afternoon. I promise. I don't know why I haven't gone before now."

"Money, I'd guess," Mattie said. "What about the baby's daddy? Has he got any?"

"Oh, he doesn't know anything about this. Nobody does. I just figured I wouldn't mention it until I had to. There was always the chance I'd have a miscarriage or get run over by a bus and never have to explain anything to anybody."

"I think you need a friend right now as much as anybody ever did," Mattie said. "Would it help to talk about it?"

Did Mattie mean talk to *her*? I didn't even know her. If I'd been inclined to talk about my situation with anybody, it would have been with T. Peter. Junior Lee, maybe. But I wasn't so inclined. Did she think that just because she was a woman, I'd confide in her?

Mattie said, "You know those collages downstairs? *One Spot of Red: Nos. 33* and *34*?"

"Yes."

"I made those. I come in here not just to eat but to visit my pictures. There's an *M* in toothpicks in *No. 33* and one in bobby pins in *No. 34*. That's my signature. Now you and Vivian Grady at the Grady Gallery are the only ones who know that."

What was this supposed to be, some kind of a

trade? She told me about her pictures, so I had to tell her about my baby?

There was something in those pictures, though. An energy, a curiosity that made me sure they hadn't been made by an ordinary person. But, no matter how extraordinary she was, why should I tell her anything?

"What I'm saying," Mattie said, interrupting my thoughts, "is that I know how to keep a secret. And I also know something about how the world works. I might be able to help you."

"Why would you want to?" I asked.

Looking at Mattie's paint-stained overalls, I also wondered how much help she could be to me if she couldn't even provide herself with clean clothes.

"Good question. And I haven't got a quick answer. It just feels like something I want to do, and one thing I've learned is to listen to my urges. There's usually a reason for them, even if I don't find out what it is until later."

Somehow that reasoning must have made sense to me, because I heard myself say, "I don't know if I ever thought I was in love with him, but now I know for sure I wasn't. What I wanted was for him to love me. Really love me."

I told her everything—about Pop and Mama and the boys; about Scott and Susan and Charlie's; about my college hopes and my fears about the future; even about how angry I sometimes felt with the baby for depriving me of so much and for maybe getting a better, luckier life than I'd had.

Once I'd started, I couldn't stop. Fainting seemed to have unlocked my resistance and tenacious de-

tachment and opened a door to my fear and lone-
liness. All Mattie had to do was walk in. And she
just listened. Maybe she asked a couple of questions,
but mostly she listened as if I were telling her the
most interesting story in the world.

When I finished, Mattie was quiet for a moment
and then said, "You're quite a girl."

Praise for getting pregnant and running away
from home seemed undeserved. But, oddly, I did
feel better for having spilled my secrets to Mattie;
less tight and tense, less frightened.

"I'm worried about this fainting spell of yours,"
she said. "I'd guess it's mostly fatigue and anxiety,
but you definitely need checking."

"I know you're right. I promise I'll go to a clinic
this afternoon."

"I'll take you on my scooter."

I looked at her. "Why?"

She shrugged. "Another urge."

Having just told a stranger what I hadn't been
willing to tell Scott or Susan or T. Peter, or even,
except for a little of it, Mama, I couldn't argue with
an urge. I just said, "Okay."

I went downstairs to the Gourmaniac with Mattie, who explained to T. Peter that she was taking
me to a clinic to be checked over.

"Is that okay with you, Daphne?" he asked. After
all, he didn't know any more about Mattie than I
did. "I definitely think you should get to a clinic,
but I could take you after closing."

"It's okay, T. Peter. I'll be fine with Mattie. I just
hate to leave before closing."

"It's only another half hour. Anyway, you're more important than a few people waiting for their lunch. Go ahead. Take tomorrow off, too."

I impulsively kissed his cheek, and we left. I could see him standing in the doorway of the Gourmaniac, watching us the whole time I was arranging myself on the back of Mattie's scooter. I waved to him as we took off.

The rain had stopped, and the brief ride in the cool, damp air was exhilarating. The clinic wasn't crowded, and I was seen right away. The doctor stuck strictly to my medical history and didn't ask me any personal questions. The exam was awkward and embarrassing, but at least it didn't hurt, and I was relieved finally to be forced out of my lethargy and into doing something I knew I had to do.

Then I waited with Mattie for the test results.

About five o'clock, the doctor called me back and told me, "Everything looks good with the baby. You're a bit anemic and a little underweight." He handed me a bottle of iron pills. "Take one of these every day, get some rest and more to eat, and come back in a month."

"That's a relief," Mattie said when I told her what the doctor had said. "Let me buy you some dinner, and then I'll take you home."

"You don't have to buy me dinner." I expected nothing more from her. She'd turned out to be the perfect person to tell my story to, and that was enough.

"I want to," Mattie said. "Come on."

# SIXTEEN

O ver dinner I was too tired to talk much, and
besides, I'd told Mattie everything I had to
tell that afternoon. So Mattie talked about herself.

"It's funny how families run out," she said. "My
father was an only child. Pale and sickly and pitiful.
Nobody thought he'd live long enough to get married, and even if he did marry, he wouldn't know
what a husband was supposed to do. And when he
went, that branch of the Burneys would be finished.
Well, he fooled everybody.

"When he was forty-five he married my mother,
who was every bit as pale and sickly and pitiful as
he was, and a thirty-three-year-old spinster to boot.
In the next ten years they had seven kids, so I guess
they weren't all *that* sickly. So here the Burneys
were, a whole big family again, new lease on life,
ought to go on forever.

"Not only that, but every one of those seven Burney babies weighed at least eight pounds, and most
of us grew up tough and scrappy and mean as home-

made sin. Well, two of us died before we could get married, three of us, including me, never got married at all, and the two that did didn't produce any offspring. So here we are, right back where we started, ready to run out. Only me and one sister left."

"Why didn't you get married?" I asked. Having told her my secrets, I felt entitled to ask for a few of hers.

"Never found a man I liked better than I liked myself," she said. "Well, there was one, but he married my sister Geneva, the only one besides me who's still alive. William and I were a pretty hot item for a while, but Geneva's a natural born nurturer and he figured she'd take better care of him than I would. And he was right. I had too many other things I wanted to do. I couldn't see staying home to darn socks and make corned beef and cabbage the way Geneva did. So she got him."

"Were you ever sorry?"

"Oh, sure. I took off for New York to study art and get away from them. You should have seen those first canvases. So full of rage and bitterness. Just big slashes of color struck with an angry hand. But, after a while, I took comfort in my painting, and it saved me.

"I had friends, too, and some distracting love affairs—you wouldn't think so to look at me now, but I was real exceptional-looking once." I thought she was still pretty exceptional. "So I got over it and started figuring out how to make my own life. It was just getting interesting when I had to go home to take care of my parents.

"They were both still pale and sickly and pitiful and difficult as could be. Just *wouldn't* lie down and die for the longest time. It's ironic it was me who ended up taking care of them. Geneva would have loved it, only she was too far away and had William to look after. I was the logical one, being so rootless, but I was the least suited to it.

"Eventually, though, my father died, and my mother not too long after that. I can't say I was sorry. By the end, they were so querulous and demanding, I was lying awake nights, thinking up the perfect murder.

"They left me the house, certainly more house than I'll ever need, and some money; and by the time they were gone, I was forty-four years old and had found a little peace. I threw myself into my art then, and for the last fifteen years that's about all I've done. Life can get cluttered if you let it. It's important to get focused. You've got to concentrate your energy."

"The one spot of red!" I said. "That's what it means."

Mattie smiled at me. "I knew you were a smart girl the first time I laid eyes on you."

"I was sure that spot of red meant something. It had to, but I didn't know what. Now it makes sense. You have to figure out what's most important to you, and put the other stuff in the background." I felt as excited as I had when I'd first seen the pictures.

"Well, it took me a long time to get there myself. The money my parents left me started running out after a while. I didn't want to sell the house—old as it is, it's home—and I didn't want to take in boarders. Too much trouble. And God knows I didn't want to have to get a job.

"One day, I passed by the Grady Gallery, and in the window I saw an unusual painting—not your typical seascape, or fake impressionist, or abstract done by a talented chimpanzee. So I went home and got a few of my things—by then I had years' worth of pictures filling up the upstairs bedrooms— and I took them to Vivian Grady and she liked them.

"She's sold almost everything I've produced, and she protects my privacy. I need peace to do my work. I've got quite a name as an artist—only it isn't my real name. I paint under M. Bush—from that nursery song 'Here we go round the mulberry bush.' At least it's my real initials."

"How come you're telling me this if nobody else knows?"

"Maybe it's just like I said, I follow my urges. Maybe it's time I told somebody. The same way you told me your secret. I really don't know, but a reason usually makes itself known sooner or later, and I expect this one will, too."

"I won't tell anybody," I said. "I can keep a secret." I sipped some tea. "I wish I knew what my spot of red was."

"It can be different things at different times in your life. Maybe right now it's that baby. Some people never do seem to figure it out, though."

I was afraid I'd be one of them. Either I'd never figure out just what I wanted or, if I did, I'd never be able to get it.

"I've been rattling on like a senile old poop," she

said, "and you so tired you're sagging. Come on, I'm taking you home."

When Mattie brought the motorbike to a stop in front of the YWCA she asked, "You live here? For how long?"

I was yawning too widely to speak, but when I could, I said, "Almost two months, I guess. Why?"

"Is this where you intend to stay?"

"Is there something wrong with that? It may be dingy, but it's cheap and it's close to the Gourmaniac. You should have seen where I was staying before."

"I'm not sure this place is much of an improvement. This is not the best neighborhood, you know."

"There's a guard at the door."

"Huh," Mattie said, unimpressed. "What kind of people stay here?"

"Women and children. It's a YWCA, Mattie." I was starting to feel defensive. "No one stays too long. I've been here longer than anybody."

"That's the idea, child. This is a way station. You move on as soon as you can. It's not a place to live. Especially for a nice girl like you."

"Mattie, I'm pregnant and I'm not married, and I'm seventeen, remember? Doesn't sound like a nice girl to me."

Mattie braced her legs on either side of the motorbike and drew herself up. "Now you stop that right now. None of that has anything to do with how nice you are. Everybody makes mistakes, and everybody's made at least one biggie. I probably shouldn't have let Geneva have William. It's just that some people's mistakes, uh, show more." I could see the laugh lines around Mattie's eyes deepen in the streetlight's glow. "Sorry. No pun intended."

I patted Mattie's slickered arm. "Thank you. For everything. And I promise, your secret's safe." I knew, somehow, that mine was safe with her, too.

"Good night."

# SEVENTEEN

The next morning I could hardly believe the day before had happened. My fainting had fractured it into two separate and absolutely different parts: in the morning I had been myself, the self I'd gotten used to since I'd been in Lincoln, my layer of reserve and control barely containing my fear and anger. In the afternoon, with Mattie, I'd been somebody else—a person with *no* reserve or control who, with the slightest encouragement, had told a total stranger everything about herself. And Mattie had just listened with no judgment or censure, only understanding. She had said it would help to talk about it and she was right.

I couldn't stand the idea of spending the day alone so I zipped up my jeans as far as they would go, tied my apron over the gap, and went to work. It had stopped raining, but the air was cool and moist.

"I didn't think we'd see you today," T. Peter said

as I came in the door of the Gourmaniac. "You sure you're okay?"

"What are you doing here?" Junior Lee asked, coming out of the kitchen. "Don't you trust me and the chief? We only mixed up about thirty orders yesterday."

"What happened at the clinic?" T. Peter asked.

"Come on, you guys, I'm fine." I began setting tables. "I was just tired. It's nothing. And no, I don't trust you to manage without me."

Mattie came in about eleven-thirty, as usual, and T. Peter kissed her hand as he seated her. "Mattie, you're a saint."

She gave his shoulder a little shove and pulled her hand away from his, but she was smiling. "Don't be ridiculous. I only do what I want to do."

"Then I'm glad that's what you wanted to do."

"Just fill my mug with hot tea, will you? It's cold out there."

"With excessive pleasure." He bowed to her, and she gave him another little shove.

I delivered her tea, and when I set it down on the table, Mattie asked, "How do you feel today?"

"Good. Much better. Thanks again for yesterday."

"Forget it. Look, Daphne, I know you'll be busy soon with lunch, but I want you to think about something."

"Sure. What?"

"I want you to think about coming to live with me—until the baby arrives and you decide what you want to do next."

That was the last thing I expected her to say, and for a moment I was too surprised to speak. Then I asked, "But what about your peace and quiet? Your painting? Wouldn't I get in the way?"

"I think we could work it out." Mattie looked at me with her serious brown eyes. "It could be good for both of us. Just think it over."

Would it be good for me? I had no idea how she lived. It might be worse than the Y. Even if she lived in a palace, how would my living there be good for her?

"All right. If you're sure you mean it."

"I am."

After closing, T. Peter and Junior Lee made me sit down while they cleaned up and fixed lunch. T. Peter brewed me a pot of herbal tea, and Junior Lee massaged my shoulders.

"Please, you guys," I said. "I'm fine. Stop fussing."

"No way," Junior Lee said. "You got to put up with it whether you like it or not."

"Okay, Daphne," T. Peter said, sitting down and resting his chin in his palm. "It's time to level."

"Level?" My breath caught in my throat.

"Honey, I'm a doctor. I heard two heartbeats with that stethoscope yesterday. And you're not gaining weight from my good cooking."

"Oh." It was inevitable. Eventually one or the other of them had to figure it out, but I was still unprepared. "You noticed."

"It's hard to miss when you start fainting on the customers. Now, is there any kind of help we can give you?"

"Help?"

"Daphne, dear, don't be obtuse," T. Peter said. "Don't you trust us enough to talk to us? What do we have to do, make blood pledges?"

"Yeah, Daffy," Junior Lee added. "I thought we were family."

All of a sudden, my eyes were full of tears that streamed down my cheeks. Appalled, I put my head in my hands. Tears ran through my fingers and hit the table with little splats.

"Please, Daphne," T. Peter said. "Anybody could be looking in. It's not good for a restaurant's reputation to have people sitting around crying."

"Yeah," Junior Lee said. "It could be the food making you act like that."

I cried harder and got the hiccups. Junior Lee pounded me on the back, which only made the hiccups worse. He brought me a glass of water, which he spilled on me, and between the crying and the hiccuping, I could hardly catch my breath. Finally Junior Lee poured sugar in a teaspoon and stuck it in my mouth. I swallowed it without thinking, and the hiccups stopped, as if turned off by a switch. The crying slowed down, too.

"It never fails," Junior Lee said. "My Aunt Clementine taught me that. I learned a lot of good stuff from her. Like, you sleep better if your head's pointed north. You can sharpen a knife by rubbing it against a clay flowerpot. Club soda removes bloodstains. You can wash grease off your hands with sugar. Though why you'd have sugar and not soap has always wondered me."

"It was the knives and the bloodstains I was worrying about," T. Peter said.

"Just an occupational hazard," Junior Lee said.

"What did she *do?*" I asked, distracted.

Junior Lee laughed. "Nothing as good as what you're probably thinking. She worked at the Market Basket—as a butcher—to support us. Let me tell you, Daffy, I didn't have a father at home, and it's not a requirement. Now, I don't know what your situation is, though I'm pretty sure you don't have a husband, but I can tell you, all a child has to have is somebody to love them. I had Aunt Clementine, and she was plenty good enough."

"This baby will have a father. And a mother. Adopted ones," I said, blowing my nose on a napkin T. Peter handed me.

"You're giving it up?" Junior Lee asked.

"I don't see that I have a choice."

"The father agrees?" T. Peter asked.

"He doesn't know, and I'll never tell him."

"What about your family?" T. Peter asked.

"My father says I can't come home." Fresh tears started and T. Peter handed me another napkin.

"What about a home for unwed mothers? Do they still have places like that?" T. Peter said.

"I tried that. I couldn't find one where I could get in. There wasn't anything else I could think of but to go away by myself. I can manage. I'm brave. I won't be dependent on anybody."

"Allowing someone to help you is different from being dependent, Daphne," T. Peter said.

"It feels the same to me. It even makes me nervous that Mattie wants me to live with her until the baby comes."

"Mattie offered that?" T. Peter asked, looking astonished. "Why?"

"She doesn't like where I live. She says it's not a

nice neighborhood. At least the Y is better than the Hotel Edison."

"You stayed at the Hotel *Edison?*" Junior Lee asked.

"Just for one night. Why? What's wrong with it?"

"You know the guy at the desk, Kayo?"

"He's a friend of yours? I'm sorry, but he gave me the creeps."

"He's no friend of mine. Your instincts were right, Daffy. He's been in every kind of trouble you can name, and the law's only caught him at it once or twice. He wouldn't know a scruple if he found one in his pocket. That was no place for you. Especially with a baby on the way. And I agree with Mattie, the Y's not a whole lot better. Believe me, I know this area better than any of you."

"Now, Daphne," T. Peter said, rubbing his balding head and pacing to the counter and back, "maybe you should leave the Y, but as for going to Mattie's—she's a nice lady—she's got a regular's mug, after all—but we don't really know anything about her."

I couldn't tell him anything about *One Spot of Red: Nos. 33* and *34.* I'd promised.

"What would she expect from you in this arrangement?" T. Peter went on. "You don't even know where she lives. I mean, look at her. Those dirty overalls. She could spend her nights in a doorway, for all you know." He knelt beside my chair. "You know, don't you, that if you really need a place to go, you can stay with me."

"Oh," I said, and buried my face in the napkin again.

"It might be hard to explain to the neighbors,"

he said, "but since I haven't got any neighbors, no problem."

"She's got a house," I said from behind the napkin.

Junior Lee was on his knees by the other side of my chair. "Come on, Daffy. You know the harder something is, the better I like it. Let me help, too."

"Listen," T. Peter said. "It's not smart to go into any kind of a deal blind. Will you do one thing for Junior Lee and me?"

"What?" I asked, sniffling.

"Let us go with you to look at Mattie's house. Just let us see what she's got to offer you. Then we can talk about this again, you and me and Junior Lee. Okay? Will you do that?"

I thought about it for a moment before saying "All right."

He patted my knee. "Thank you. That's our girl."

# EIGHTEEN

On Sunday, I looked up the Grady Gallery in the phone book and went there on the bus. It was located in a fashionable section of town, a section of flossy boutiques, expensive little restaurants, and smart high-rise apartment buildings.

The gallery's windows were rimmed with bands of silver, and in the center of them, rotating slowly on motorized pedestals, were sculptures made of some silver-coated metal.

I hesitated at the door, self-conscious about my jeans, so worn they were almost white, my jogging shoes, and my ski jacket pulled over the gap of my unclosed zipper. Oh, well, they can't throw me out for looking, I thought as I pushed the door open and went in.

It was as quiet as a museum inside. The carpet was dark gray and the walls were pale gray with spotlighted paintings hung on them. The few customers spoke in whispers. It was a serious place.

I tiptoed around the gallery, looking at the pictures. The ones I liked most had three dimensions—paint laid on thick as frosting, swirls of ivory paper in humps and waves, human faces of papier-mâché protruding from canvas. I wanted to run my hands over them.

Then I came to Mattie's work: two small collages, different from the ones at the Gourmaniac in that they were composed of many kinds of the same item, instead of being heaped with assorted articles. One had brushes: hairbrushes, toothbrushes, vegetable brushes, complexion brushes—all whited out, with a big red paintbrush in the middle.

I understood *that* spot of red.

The other collage was all jewelry, big chunky things, the kind you find at church rummage sales. Picked out in red, among all the white baubles, was a small plain ring, a wedding band.

I wondered what kind of wife Mattie might have been if she'd married William. Would she have made art of her marriage instead of making her art on canvas? Or was making art a need that transcends other arrangements?

So often, it was impossible to know if you'd made the right choice. Just choosing something—anything—made all the other possibilities wither. What if one of them would have flowered more than the one selected? How could you know it would? What if I'd stayed home? What if I'd had an abortion?

I was getting a headache.

I looked back at the jewelry collage, at the little red wedding band.

I had a feeling Mattie and I would have a lot to talk about if I went to stay with her.

On Monday, when I brought Mattie her bowl of navy-bean soup, she said, "Why don't you come look at my house before you make up your mind? See if you think it's an improvement over the Y."

We decided on Thursday afternoon for the visit, but somehow I couldn't tell her that Junior Lee and T. Peter would be coming with me. I was afraid she would be offended.

I sat next to the bus window, holding on tightly to the back of the seat in front of me, with Junior Lee beside me and T. Peter in the seat across the aisle.

"Turn loose of that thing," Junior Lee said to me, "before you cause us to have to buy a new one."

I let go of the back of the seat as if it were hot. "Sorry. I guess I'm a little nervous."

"No kidding," Junior Lee said. "You could have fooled me."

T. Peter leaned across the aisle. "Relax, Daphne. There's nothing to worry about. Junior Lee's whole body is a lethal weapon, and I'm armed with all the wit and charm allowed by law. What can happen? If she lives in a packing crate, we'll just bop back to the Gourmaniac and work on Plan B."

"What *is* Plan B, chief?" Junior Lee asked.

"Being my roommate, the thing nine out of ten thinking women want to do."

"I always heard you could lie with statistics," Junior Lee said. "Now I know it's true."

\* \* \*

We got off the bus on a wide avenue lined with mature trees. A cold wind blew through their leafless branches, and I dug my fists into my jacket pockets. Big old houses, some with spacious front porches, sat back from the street across unkempt lawns that reminded me of my own home, littered as they were with toys or tools or piles of dead leaves. Multiple mailboxes on the fronts of some of the houses indicated that they had been cut up into apartments. Two or three seemed in the process of being restored, and one bore a sign on the door reading LAW OFFICES.

"This must have been a prime residential area once," T. Peter said. "Makes sense. Close to downtown, in the days before everyone fell in love with suburbs and automobiles."

"Looks like some folks are trying to turn it around," Junior Lee said, gesturing toward the LAW OFFICES sign. That house sported new paint, its gingerbread details highlighted with different shades of green and blue.

We walked along, looking for the address Mattie had given me, passing a small mom-and-pop market and a house with peeling paint where two children argued over a toy on the porch. We stopped next to a dark café with DEW DROP INN on its window.

"It's across the street," I said, checking the slip of paper in my hand. We crossed and stood together in front of Mattie's house: a big white Victorian one with a shiny black iron fence around the small neat yard. An English walnut tree, its leaves dropping, grew inside the fence. Every window was covered with white blinds.

"I feel like I'm in a Walt Disney movie," T. Peter said.

"I don't know what I was expecting," I said, "but this wasn't it."

Junior Lee just stared.

We mounted the shallow steps onto the encircling porch, and I twisted the doorbell, a bright brass curlicue. The front door, with its lace-curtained panel of leaded glass, opened and Mattie stood there in sneakers and overalls, her hair straggling out of its bun, white paint on her hands.

"Daphne," she said. Then she registered T. Peter and Junior Lee and blinked. She stood looking at them in silence for a moment before she said, "I never thought to ask if you'd be coming alone."

"I should have told you," I said. "I'm sorry."

"Don't be upset with Daphne," T. Peter said. "The three of us are a team. A young woman alone in a big city needs someone to count on. We're it."

"I don't have much experience with teams," Mattie said, "but if you all go together, then you better all come in." She opened the door wider, and we stepped into the broad front hall.

I felt as if I'd fallen down the rabbit hole. The inside of Mattie's old house was airy and light, nothing like the cluttered, dark interior I'd expected to see. The walls were white and hung with paintings; the shiny wood floors were bare. The only furnishings in the square hall were a leafy tree in a big white tub and a white cast-iron cat sitting beside it.

Mattie saw me looking at them. "The tree's not real, and neither is the cat. I'm the only living thing in this house. And now you three."

She opened the double arched doors that led off the hall into another large, white, sparsely furnished room. A bay window held a window seat padded in rough white cotton. In front of the fireplace two sofas in the same white fabric faced each other, with a big glass coffee table on a furry white rug between them. A leather-and-chrome chair was the only other piece of furniture in the room. Here, too, paintings covered the walls.

"I stripped away the clutter as soon as the house was mine," Mattie said. "All this space clears my mind. But I kept everything. The upstairs is full of horsehair sofas and Tiffany lamps and gimcracks and knickknacks by the carload. Just in case I ever change my mind. Sit down. I'll get us some tea."

As soon as she left the room, Junior Lee swooned onto the sofa. "Zounds, Daffy, our bag lady is an impostor. What do you suppose she does for a living? You think she's in the drug trade? No. Not Mattie. Some kind of clean crime—industrial espionage, maybe."

"Maybe she's an eccentric heiress," T. Peter said, walking around studying the paintings on the walls.

Mattie's work was so distinctive, I didn't see how he could avoid recognizing they were hers. But I'd promised I'd keep her secret, so I didn't say anything.

"I've never been in a house like this," I said, sitting carefully on the other white sofa.

"Can Daffy be happy living in the lap of luxury with an eccentric heiress for her landlady?" Junior Lee asked. "What do you think, chief?"

"Looks good to me," he said. "What do you think, Daphne?"

"It might work," I said hesitantly. "But if I come, I think I should pay rent. Keep it businesslike. Then I won't feel obligated."

"Daffy, think about it. Sometimes you should let people do things for you." Junior Lee leapt up from his sofa to sit next to me. "It's like a gift. You don't pay people for presents they give you. Not everything needs to be businesslike."

"But it makes me uncomfortable. Why should she want to do this?"

"I don't know. Maybe you'll find out and maybe you won't. But Mattie doesn't look like the kind of lady to make an offer like this if she didn't mean it. I bet it'd be pretty hard to make Mattie do something she didn't want to do."

T. Peter said, "I say this looks like a great spot for you. Better than Plan B, that's for sure."

Mattie came through the arched doorway with a big white tray holding a white teapot and cups, and a red glass plate of thin round chocolate cookies. She smelled of turpentine, and her hands were clean of paint.

"You did the collages at the Gourmaniac, didn't you?" T. Peter asked. "Is that why you come in there?"

Mattie set the tray on the coffee table. "Daphne knew. I didn't know you'd be coming with her today."

"I'm sorry," I said miserably. "I didn't tell anybody, but I never thought—"

"Too late now," Mattie said, pouring a cup of tea and handing it to T. Peter. "But as long as you know my secret, I hope you'll keep it."

"Why all the mystery?" T. Peter asked, taking the cup.

"I like my privacy. I work better that way. And I waited a long time to have things the way I want them. It's important."

"Your secret's safe with us." He gently kicked Junior Lee in the ankle. "Right?"

"Oh, sure. Right, chief. Who am I going to tell, anyway?"

Mattie poured more tea and passed the cookies, which T. Peter fingered lovingly. "My favorite shape."

"Your house is beautiful," I said. Even if she'd changed her mind about having me stay, I wanted her to know how much I liked her house.

"Mind telling me what you were expecting?" Mattie asked.

Junior Lee and T. Peter and I exchanged glances, and I said, "We guessed everything from a packing crate to an open doorway. I knew you were a successful artist, but I still expected something a little . . . grubbier. More bohemian."

Mattie shook her head. "I couldn't live like that. I've tried it. I need order. I'm guessing you're that way, too, just from the way you work at the Gourmaniac. If you're not, I'll teach you."

Did that mean she still wanted me?

"No. I like things neat, too. Even if I didn't, I wouldn't have the nerve to mess up this place."

"I think we can get along fine. Anyway, it won't last forever. Just until the baby comes and you decide what happens next. You need a place to stay, and I'm finally tired of being alone all the time."

So she hadn't changed her mind. Still, I hesitated. Could I keep my independence, living so closely with another person? It hadn't been easy at home. But living alone hadn't been so easy either. Well, why shouldn't I enjoy Mattie's pretty house for a while? I could always leave if it didn't work out. "Okay. If you all think it's such a good idea, I guess I do, too."

"You had me worried there for a minute, Daffy," Junior Lee said.

"When would you like me to come?" I asked. "I pay by the day at the Y, so I can come whenever you—"

"Nonsense. Come tomorrow, of course."

T. Peter put his cup on the table and stood up. "We should get going before the rush hour gets started. Looks like rain again, too. I hope you won't mind if Junior Lee and I come to see Daphne from time to time. Ours is more than a professional relationship."

He was right. Both he and Junior Lee were involved with my real life now.

Mattie got up, too. "What the hell," she said. "Why fool around, dipping my toes in the water. I might as well get wet."

"What?" T. Peter asked.

"Why don't you and Junior Lee come have dinner with me and Daphne Sunday night? I don't want to go breaking up a team."

# NINETEEN

T. Peter and Junior Lee got off the bus before I did, so I was alone when I returned to the YWCA. After I had been in Mattie's beautiful house, the Y looked worse than usual to me. The rooms were clean enough, but nowhere was there evidence that someone cared about making the surroundings pleasing to the eye. Basic comforts were provided—adequate blankets, enough drawer space, hot water—but there was no provision for the comforts of the spirit—a welcoming voice, the touch of a friendly hand, a fireplace to gather near. These were things I was pretty sure I would find at Mattie's; things I was determined to relish and resist at the same time.

I packed my bag, which didn't take long, leaving out only my clothes for the next day, my toothbrush and my hairbrush. Library books were stacked beside the bag, to be returned on my way to Mattie's.

It wasn't late but it was winter-dark outside, and I was tired. I lay listening to the traffic on the street and feeling the baby roll within me. What sounds would I be hearing tomorrow night? What bed would I be sleeping in? I wished I'd asked to see the room that would be mine before I'd left Mattie's. What bed would I be sleeping in after Mattie's?

By the time I'd finished cleaning up at the Gourmaniac, returned my library books, and taken the bus to Mattie's, daylight was fading and a fine, drizzly mist blurred the streetlights.

I stood on Mattie's porch for several moments before I raised my hand to the doorbell. I'd barely had time to hear the faint sound of the ring before the door opened.

Mattie wore paint-spattered overalls. "I was trying to work while I waited for you, but I kept thinking about you coming and I couldn't concentrate."

"I'm sorry."

"No, no. It's me. I want to do this, and I want to do it right, and I'm afraid I won't know how. I've lived alone so long, I've forgotten how to be gracious. Maybe I never was. I probably wasn't. Geneva never thought so. She was the gracious one. After you left, I realized I hadn't let you choose your bedroom. There are lots of rooms upstairs, but I keep them all closed so I don't have to heat them. Anyway, they're full of furniture from downstairs. But there are three bedrooms down here. One's mine, of course, the biggest one, but a feeling of space is very important to me." Then she stopped talking and shook her head disgustedly. "Listen to me. Nervous as a schoolgirl. Come in." She closed the door behind me. "I'm glad you're here. There's a fire in the front room. Let's go in there."

I followed her through the arched doorway.

"Do you mind if we don't turn on the lamps?" Mattie asked. "This is my favorite time of day. I love to watch the light change."

"Sure. It's your house. You don't have to ask me."

"I'm trying to be gracious," she said, smiling.

Mattie sat down, and I sat on the sofa facing her, my bag on the floor beside me.

"Changing times are the most interesting times, even though they're usually the hardest, too, don't you think?" Mattie said. "They're the times you remember."

"You mean like now, for me?"

"For me, too."

"Maybe someday I'll think it was interesting. I don't believe I'll have any trouble remembering it."

"Probably not." Mattie leaned her head against the back of the couch. I watched her in the dwindling light, and did the same. Raindrops hit the windows with tiny pinging sounds. If Junior Lee had been there, I could have told him that now I felt *hors de combat*, too. I didn't think I could get up if the house was on fire. The shadows in the room deepened. The only sounds were the settling of logs in the fireplace, and the rain. I closed my eyes.

When I woke up, the room was completely dark except for the dying fire. A moment passed before I knew where I was. As I squinted in the darkness, trying to locate a lamp, I heard footsteps and looked up to see Mattie silhouetted in the doorway.

"So you're awake now. Good. Dinner's ready."

I turned on a lamp and looked more closely at her. She wore red slacks, a loose white silk shirt, and red combs in her hair. "You look terrific," I said.

"One of the ways I separate work life from home life: by changing clothes. It's hard to keep them separate when you work at home. Come on. Let's get you cleaned up and fed, and then we'll find you a place to sleep."

Mattie led me down the hall to a big, white-tiled bathroom with a claw-footed tub and red towels. I washed my face and finger-combed my hair. I looked at myself closely in the mirror, but I could see none of the changes in my life on my face. Even my hair was growing back.

I found my way to the dining room—another big white room, furnished with a golden oak table and walls full of art—where Mattie sat waiting for me.

"I should warn you," she said. "I don't cook. I can—at least I *think* I still can, it's been so long since I've tried—I just don't like to." Between the two place settings was a platter of fruit, nuts, sliced meat, and cheese. A bottle of wine and a basket of bread stood next to it. "Sit down."

I did.

Mattie said, "A long time ago I saw a Russian movie—I've forgotten the name of it—and every time the characters sat down to eat, this is what they had: cheese and bread and fruit. And I thought, What a great idea. Everything you need, and it's so easy. So I survive on this and deli food—and the Gourmaniac, of course. I don't have beriberi yet.

The kitchen's at your disposal if you want something else."

Living the way Mattie lived seemed so alien to me, I felt as though I'd stepped into another universe. I'd always thought there were rules people had to live by, several of which I'd already broken and didn't know how to mend. But Mattie had made her own rules.

"I never thought of living without cooking," I said.

"There are a lot of things people do without thinking," Mattie said. "Usually, you don't do much thinking until you come up against something you don't like. Then you can grit your teeth and put up with it, or you can try to find a way around it. I always hated cooking. When my parents got so old and sick, I was forever making custards and cream soups and little delicacies they wanted, and I felt as if I had to do that. They were on the way out, and it wasn't fair of me to make it hard for them. Once they were gone, though, I felt like sawing the kitchen right off the house and eating every meal out. But that was too expensive, and there were times when the weather was too bad or I was too lazy or too undressed or too sick to go out, so it made sense to keep a kitchen attached to the house, but to find a way to stay out of it as much as possible."

"My mother's a good cook, but I don't think she likes it very much. Gardening is her favorite way to be creative."

"I should have known about the garden. That's why you're Daphne."

I nodded. "Most people don't know Daphne's a plant."

"Kind of old-fashioned, but it's a very pretty name." She took a swallow of her wine. "Well, I like to see people being creative. To my mind, being creative is doing something *once*. I make each picture one time. They're all different. I must have made custard four hundred times. That's creating, but it's not creative."

Mattie passed me the platter and poured herself more wine. "Would you like some?"

I had never had wine with a meal before. I nodded.

"You've got some of that, you know," Mattie said, filling my glass.

"Some of what?"

"A creative approach to living. You must have put a lot of thought into it before you did something as extreme as leaving home."

"I don't know. It felt impulsive. Sometimes I wonder . . ." I sipped the wine. The taste was strange, almost bitter, and I didn't like it. It probably wasn't good for the baby, either.

"Well, you decided not to have an abortion, you left home with every intention of having this baby all by yourself, with no help from anybody."

"It seemed like the only thing I could do."

"It surely was not. You *could* have had an abortion. You could have told the father. You could have told your parents. You could have stayed home. You could have gone to a home for unwed mothers. You could have jumped off a bridge . . ."

I smiled at the absurd efficiency of ending two lives at once.

". . . But you didn't. You made up your own way to do it."

She understood.

"What about later?" Mattie asked. "After the baby comes?"

That awful, unanswered question. "I don't know. There'll be a big dent in my savings, and I won't have finished high school. I may be waitressing at the Gourmaniac forever."

"But you will have ensured that the baby will be in a good place. Every baby should have a family that wants it and loves it and is willing to do all the hard things that go along with child-rearing," Mattie said. "If you can't offer that to a baby, then I think the smart thing to do is make sure the baby goes to a family that can. And I don't for one minute think that'll be easy to do."

Until she said that, I hadn't considered that it would be at all difficult. Ever since I'd found out I was pregnant, all I'd wanted to do was get rid of the problem. But suddenly I realized that somewhere along the line I'd stopped thinking of it as just a baby. It was *my* baby. That was the last thing in the world I wanted to think, when my life was already so complicated. How had Mattie known?

She just looked at me and said, "Wouldn't it be nice if every problem had a neat solution that was easy and never hurt anybody?"

"Yes," I said faintly. "That would be wonderful."

"Well, it doesn't happen in real life. Oh, maybe once in a while, if you've been very, very good and are very, very lucky. Not something you'd want to count on."

"No," I said. "I know that."

Mattie finished her wine and stretched. "Well, we're not going to change the way the world works, even if we sit here all night. Let's get you a bedroom now. One nice thing about dinners like this is that there aren't any pots to scrub."

Mattie showed me two empty bedrooms at the back of the house. They were both big and roomy, but I picked the corner one because there were windows on two walls and I thought it would be brighter. Also, the head of the bed pointed north.

"I'll leave you alone now to get settled," Mattie said. "If you want, and the weather cooperates, tomorrow after work you can go gathering with me."

"Gathering?"

"Looking for stuff for the collages. The rain's kept me in and my stock's getting low. Good night." She closed the door, and I heard her footsteps going down the hall.

My new room was quite a change from the Y. The double bedstead was white iron, and there was a patchwork quilt on the bed. A white wicker rocker sat next to a marble-topped chest of drawers, and one of Mattie's collages hung on the wall.

I put my things into the dresser drawers. When I came upon the slim bundle of Scott's letters in the bottom of my bag, I hesitated before finally putting them into the drawer. Then I climbed into the high bed, pulled the thick blanket up to my chin, turned out the light, and lay with my hand over my moving baby until I fell asleep.

# TWENTY

The next day was gray and windy but without rain.

Mattie came into the Gourmaniac for her soup at eleven-thirty, and then returned to get me just as I was finishing lunch with T. Peter and Junior Lee. She brought a pair of overalls for me to change into, and they were a lot more comfortable than my unzipped jeans. We went on the motorbike to the neighborhood of Vivian Grady's gallery, to the alleys behind and alongside the fancy apartment buildings where the big trash containers were.

Mattie stopped her bike, pulled on a pair of rubber gloves, unhooked a stick about the length of a pool cue from the side of the bike, and began poking around in the trash.

I watched and held my nose. "Ugh! How can you stand the smell? There *must* be another way to do this."

"You get used to it. I think it's very interesting. If I hadn't gotten into art, I might have made a good garbageologist."

"What in the world is a garbageologist?"

"Somebody who figures out social customs from people's leavings."

"I thought those were anthropologists."

"Same thing. I've sure found some stories in the trash. Once, I found a whole wedding outfit—dress, shoes, veil, garter, the works—in a plastic bag. I've always wondered if it was pitched before or after the wedding. Jilted or disappointed?"

Mattie fished out a chipped teacup and put it in a plastic bag. Then she went back to stirring the trash around in the bin. "Another time I found a pile of love letters tied with a green ribbon—all typewritten, addressed to Michelle."

"Did you read them?"

"It's funny. I took them home, but it was a long time before I read them. It felt so much like . . . I don't know . . . trespassing. Violating somebody's privacy."

"But Michelle threw them away. She didn't want them."

"I finally justified it that way. And I was curious about somebody who'd type love letters."

"Maybe his handwriting was illegible—he could have been a doctor. Maybe he had arthritis. Or they were anonymous. What did they say?"

"They all said the same thing. 'Michelle, I love you. Love, Paul.' No imagination. No wonder Michelle tossed them out."

I couldn't help thinking of Scott's bland letters as I watched Mattie pull a couple of broken barrettes, a flashlight battery, and a bunch of yellow plastic flowers out of the bin.

After observing the uncommon pleasure Mattie took in rummaging around in garbage cans, I decided to see what it was all about. At the next stop, I put on the extra pair of rubber gloves she had brought, took the stick from her, and, holding my nose with one hand, gingerly poked around in the trash. I knew what I'd always thought when I saw people going through garbage cans, and I felt almost as if I should explain to passersby that what I was doing was motivated by art, not hunger. Mattie seemed unperturbed, no matter how many people stared, and finally I shrugged and went on with my trash picking. If I was going to play Mattie's game, I'd play by her rules.

I turned out to have a good feel for the kind of thing Mattie liked—a picture frame, a roller skate, a ring of keys, a typewriter cartridge.

By five o'clock, it was getting too dark to see well, but by then Mattie had a satisfyingly full pair of saddlebags and said she was ready to go home and run what treasures she could through the dishwasher.

We rode home, cold, in the early dusk, to take hot showers, change clothes, and have tea in front of the fire. Like drinking wine and sifting through garbage, tea by a fireplace was something new to me. There was no fireplace at home, and even if there had been, I couldn't see sitting by it and drinking tea from thin white cups with Pop and Mama and the boys.

"What did you do with Michelle's love letters?" I asked Mattie.

"I haven't done anything with them yet. Maybe I'll put them in a collage, and outline the words in red. Imagine her surprise if she walked by Vivian's and saw them in the window. She could probably sue me."

"What would the red mean in that collage?"

"Good question. Lately I've noticed my collages have more of a theme to them, not just heaps of junk with one random red thing to symbolize the need for focus. Now I seem to be making individual statements."

"Like the one about painting at the gallery? With all the brushes?"

"When did you see that?" Mattie asked, surprised.

"About a week ago. I knew that was about you. The red brush was you."

"So it was." She put her teacup on the coffee table, and was quiet for a moment before she leaned back again. "I don't know what I'll do about those love letters. They seem so coldhearted, so unloving, typed and repetitive like that. Maybe I'll combine them with some calculators. That's the kind of love letter you write when you've got too much mind and not enough heart. You think that's too obvious? Too corny? Too predictable?"

"What do I know?" I said, drowsily. "You're the creative one. What about the wedding ring collage? What's that about?"

"I'm not sure," Mattie answered. "Maybe it's about Geneva and William. I've been thinking about them lately. Their marriage has been her life. She's been the kind of wife every man must dream of: she's attentive, adoring, good-natured, and a great cook. I wonder what she would have done if she hadn't gotten married." She stood up. "I wonder what I'd have done if I had. Come on. Let's open a can of soup and throw together some salad."

Sunday, it rained again. I slept off and on all day, in my bed, on the couch by the fire, reading in my rocker. It was lovely to feel, even for a short time, so warm and secure and cared for. I didn't even think of Mama and the boys too often.

Mattie had picked up a tray of enchiladas from the Mexican café a block away for our dinner party that night, and then she worked all afternoon in her studio. The quiet house held peace and order, and it was impossible not to enjoy it.

# TWENTY-ONE

W hen Junior Lee and T. Peter arrived, Mattie, in a long embroidered Mexican dress and I in jeans and Mattie's loose white silk top, were setting the table with sterling flatware, thin crystal glasses, and translucent china.

"They sure make bag ladies different where I come from," Junior Lee said. "You got yourself one great disguise, Miss Mattie."

"These things belonged to my family," Mattie said, "but we hardly ever used them. My mother saved them for 'good,' which meant Christmas and birthdays. Once it was all mine, I decided to use it. To me, every day is 'good.' So I break something once in a while. Most of it'll last longer than I do, anyway."

Mattie poured a glass of wine for each of us, and then she and I brought the enchiladas to the table, along with a salad and a bowl of fruit.

"This is the roundest dinner I could think of," she said to T. Peter as we sat down. "Tell me about your love affair with the circle."

"I don't know where it comes from, but I've always had it. There's something about roundness that satisfies my soul. It's such a complete shape. Did you ever notice how many round images there are? A round of applause, of ammunition, of golf. A family circle, a vicious circle—sometimes they're the same thing—a dress circle, a circular argument. There are songs in rounds, dances in the round, theaters-in-the-round, spheres of influence. Circles are basic. I wanted a round bed when I was married, but my wife thought it was childish. Well, I have one now, even though it just about fills up my bedroom in that little apartment, and the sheets cost an arm and a leg and your firstborn child. But I've never slept better."

"Circles are your spot of red," I said.

"What?"

"Like in Mattie's pictures. The one thing that's your focus."

"Is *that* what those pictures are about? I should have guessed. What's your spot of red, Mattie?"

"Making the pictures, what else?"

"Can't you have more than one spot?" Junior Lee asked. "I couldn't tell you what mine is. I'd have to have a bunch."

"Maybe. But it's a lot harder. You need a lot of energy."

"That I got. And I want to do everything. I'd say having just one spot of red could make you a mite narrow."

"It depends on how much you like that spot of red," Mattie said. "It can be all the company you need."

T. Peter said, "I like circles well enough, but I need more than that. I guess I'd have to have more than one spot, too."

"Everybody's different," Mattie said. "I'm happy with one."

We finished the enchiladas and the wine, and took our coffee into the living room. Mattie stirred up the fire again, and put out a plate of little round cakes from the neighborhood bakery.

Junior Lee lay on the rug in front of the fire with his eyes closed. Mattie and T. Peter tried to play a game of chess with Mattie's father's alabaster chess set, but T. Peter couldn't remember the rules and kept trying to jump Mattie's pieces as if he were playing checkers. Finally Mattie conceded, saying it was hopeless to play with someone who was using the rules from some other game.

I sat on the couch, staring into the fire, without a thought in my head.

Junior Lee snored softly, and our laughter woke him up.

"Come on, tiger," T. Peter said, pulling him to his feet. "If that's all the entertainment you can provide, it's time to go home."

At the front door, T. Peter turned back to Mattie and said, "How about if I bring something from the Gourmaniac for dinner next Sunday?"

Mattie didn't answer right away. Finally she said, "If you like. It's hard for me to turn down a meal somebody else cooks."

*  *  *

T. Peter brought Swedish meatballs with new potatoes and baby beets, and after we'd chased our
rolling dinner around our plates, we agreed that
next time mashed potatoes would be a good idea,
to anchor all the round things. He also brought a
checkerboard, and taught Mattie how to play a sensible game with rules you didn't have to be a rocket
scientist to understand.

As he and Junior Lee left, Mattie reminded him,
"Mashed potatoes next Sunday, don't forget."

He didn't, and they came in handy for the codfish
balls and green peas. Mattie beat T. Peter four
games of checkers out of five, and he accused her
of snookering him. "Anybody who can play chess
probably cut her teeth on checkers, right? And after
I cooked the dinner, too. You should be ashamed of
yourself, Mattie."

It was the first time I'd ever heard Mattie giggle.
Then she went on to win three more games in a
row.

The days between the Sunday dinners were or-
derly and quiet. I worked at the Gourmaniac, and
Mattie worked in her studio. I loved our plain, simple meals together. Sometimes we talked while we
ate and sometimes we didn't, but either way, the
time felt peaceful and companionable. Once, when
I was slow to put down *For Whom the Bell Tolls* and
come to dinner, Mattie told me to bring the book
to the table. "There's no law against reading while
you eat, if it's something too good to stop." Then
she went upstairs and returned with *A Farewell to
Arms*, and we both read through the meal. A few

days later we exchanged books, and when we'd finished them, we talked about them.

For Thanksgiving, T. Peter brought a turkey he'd stuffed and roasted in the oven at the Gourmaniac. He'd suggested turkey roll for its roundness, but we had vetoed that. Not everything was better just because it was round. Mattie supplied pies from the bakery, and wine. I fixed carrot and celery sticks and opened a can of olives and one of cranberry sauce, and Junior Lee brought brown-and-serve rolls and a box of chocolates. "Chocolate's full of vitamins," he said.

After dinner, we leaned back in our chairs and loosened our belts. At least the others did. I was past the point of having a waist to belt.

"That was great," T. Peter said. "All my favorite things. My wife had this idea of what Thanksgiving dinner was supposed to be like, and she just wouldn't quit. Every year she'd fix, and then throw out, the oyster stuffing, the creamed onions, the mincemeat pie, the brussels sprouts—all this stuff she thought was proper, but which the kids and I hated. Then she'd get mad at us for not eating it. I don't miss any of it."

"Creamed onions?" Junior Lee said. "Sounds like something you have to eat for punishment."

"That's about right," T. Peter said.

"So, Daffy," Junior Lee said, shifting carefully in his chair, "when you going back to school?"

I looked at him, feeling drugged by too much food in too warm a room. "Huh?"

"You got to pay attention, Daffy. Some fancy conversation going on without you."

"Sorry. When I'm too full, my brain quits."

"That never stops me from going right on talking."

T. Peter said, "We've noticed that, time and again."

"I'm going to take that as a compliment, chief. I said, 'Daffy, when you going back to school?'"

"Oh."

"Did I say something wrong?"

"No. I just haven't thought ahead very much. I can't seem to plan past having this baby. I guess I don't really believe it'll ever happen."

"Well, I'm betting it will. Why don't you take the high school equivalency test?" he asked. "You were going to finish in January anyway, right? How much more could you have learned in five months? If you pass, you could start college in the summer and be ahead of everybody else, not behind. Even if you don't start until fall, you'd still be right where you should be."

"Hmm," I said, not able actually to confront the problem.

"If you're worried about money, you could get a loan. Or a scholarship. Or a job. Or all three. I know all about that stuff. I could help you."

"That's a great idea," Mattie said. "Why didn't I think of that? I know you could pass the test. Of course, you could. Anybody who can play checkers with T. Peter can easily pass that test. Anybody who can stand to *watch* T. Peter play checkers could probably pass it."

"Do you really think I could? I haven't been in school for months. I feel as if I've forgotten everything."

"I've seen the test, Daffy. One of the multiple-choice questions is 'How would you measure the height of a fence? With (a) a yardstick, (b) a thermometer, (c) a tablespoon, (d) a protractor?' Almost everybody picks *protractor* because it sounds the most important. You could do it easy."

Days passed and some sort of lethargy prevented me from finding out about the test. It was the same kind of lethargy that had prevented me from going to the clinic. I felt as if I were still too full of Thanksgiving dinner, still sitting in a too-warm room.

I was so lulled by the safety of being at Mattie's, I didn't want to think about it ending. I would have been perfectly content to go on forever working at the Gourmaniac, coming home to supper with Mattie, looking forward to the next Sunday dinner with T. Peter and Junior Lee, and making an occasional gathering expedition. I'd even stay pregnant forever, in spite of the heartburn, shortness of breath, and stretching skin, if I could make that lovely limbo of no demands and no fear last. Because the one thing I was sure of was that every good time ended too soon.

Only when it became clear that Junior Lee would keep on hounding me until I did something about the equivalency test did I make some phone calls and go fill out the forms. It seemed the only way to get him to leave me alone, but I resented being reminded that there was an end to this peaceful time.

"You've got to plan, Daffy," Junior Lee told me. "Nothing good happens without planning."

I believed him. But planning for my future meant

arranging to get rid of the baby, too, and thinking of that was getting harder and harder. As the baby got bigger and moved more inside me, it felt more like my own small friend. I couldn't have been more dismayed. That kind of thinking would only complicate the inevitable future.

I went to work at the Gourmaniac, and did my exercises, and studied the books recommended by the Education Office. I took naps and vitamins and tried to remember logarithms and American history. I went gathering with Mattie, rubbed lanolin onto my stretching stomach, and did practice tests until I saw them in my sleep. And in my sleep I once again listened to the racing of my heart—now, I thought, echoed by a faint baby heartbeat.

Just before Christmas, I took the test, and on Christmas morning, under a tree trimmed entirely with red ornaments, I found a present from Mattie: my equivalency certificate, framed in red.

T. Peter and Junior Lee brought Christmas brunch, arriving during the first flurries of a gentle snowstorm, and after the food was demolished, we sat by the fire, exchanging gifts. I had tins for each of them filled with cookies I'd baked. Mattie's were all red, T. Peter's were all round, and Junior Lee's were in odd assorted shapes.

Mattie gave T. Peter a collage of circles: jar lids and bottle tops, softballs and wheels from toy trucks, a round ashtray, a saucer, a Frisbee, a 45 record, and, in the center, a bright red, petrified bagel.

"Oh, my gosh, I love it, I love it," he caroled, hugging Mattie. He gave her a lifetime supply of tickets for free meals at the Gourmaniac.

She gave Junior Lee a collage with many spots of red. "You can paint them white as you narrow things down," she told him.

"You know me," he said. "I'll probably add more." He gave her a bottle of wine and some jeweled combs for her hair.

Junior Lee's gift to me was a loose dress of Indian print material, in soft blues and lavenders. I went right to my room and put it on. It was so light, its twilight-colored folds fluttered around me at the slightest movement, and I didn't feel as lumpy and graceless as I had before. Even my growing-out hair looked less ragged.

When I returned to the living room, to compliments so extravagant they made me laugh, T. Peter gave me his gift: a leather-bound volume of Emily Dickinson's poems. "You'll love them," he said, and then patted my stomach affectionately. "You're my favorite shape."

As we lay around Mattie's living room in the Christmas wreckage, Junior Lee picked up my framed certificate and put it in what was left of my lap. "This here's not the end, Daffy. It's the start."

As I was getting ready for bed, Sonny's face came into my mind, and, before I could stop it, a flood of memories of home. I knew I'd been avoiding them all day, and even longer than that—ever since I'd called home and found out I couldn't go back, no matter what happened.

Sonny was four now, and Jack would soon be six. Until now, I'd shared all their birthdays, all their Christmases, known everything about them. Who would they be when—if—I saw them again? How much could I have affected the changes in them if I'd stayed home? What changes had my leaving caused?

It was done. I couldn't think about it.

I got into bed and folded my arms across my swollen body, and wished I had a family with whom I felt as good as I did when I was with Mattie, T. Peter, and Junior Lee.

# TWENTY-TWO

I got off the bus in front of the City College bookstore, having finally given in to Junior Lee's re-
lentless insistence that I at least get a course
catalogue to look at. I stood on the sidewalk in the
cold January wind, my ski jacket open over my
stomach. A constant stream of students went into
the bookstore and came out loaded down with
books and packages.

Why hadn't I thought? It was the beginning of
the semester, the busiest time, with everybody buy-
ing books for new classes. The bookstore would be
a madhouse.

All the girls going up and down the steps seemed
lithe and long-legged, even in their winter clothes,
their hair blowing in the wind as if they were posing
for shampoo ads. They were the kind of girls I was
sure Scott was spending time with at his college.

Watching them made me feel fat and awkward
and uncertain. I pushed my hair away from my face

and, for the first time since I'd cut it, wished it was as long as it used to be.

I hadn't the nerve to go in there now, pushing my stomach ahead of me, among the crowds of students. They all looked so sure of themselves and eager and happy. I crossed the street and boarded the bus back to Mattie's, defeated and afraid.

The next week, I returned to the bookstore on my way to an appointment at the clinic. It had been a long week, full of lectures from myself and from Junior Lee, and of useless attempts at new hairstyles. I'd tried to order a course catalogue by phone, but they weren't mailed locally. I had to pick it up in person.

Weak sunshine painted my silhouette on the sidewalk in front of the bookstore. It looked like the Goodyear blimp.

I hauled myself up the steps, past bicycle racks and lockers, and went inside. There were a few students shopping, but no crowds, as there had been the week before. I roamed through the aisles the way I did in the library, touching the spines of the books, inhaling the scent of ink and paper. Here, unlike at the library, all the books were new and crisp. I loved the worn, used look of old books, too, their pages soft and ivory-colored, but the new books crackled with such tantalizing promise.

And the titles! *Women on the American Frontier, Milestones in Chemistry, The Autobiographical Impulse, Social Epidemiology, Primitive Religions, Intermediate Russian, Sleep and Dreams, African Philosophy, Germany in the Twenties, French Cinema, Marxian Economics, Neurobiology.* There was so much I didn't know anything about.

At the ends of the aisles were piles of *Bulletin: Courses of Instruction.* I took one and meant to leave then, but as I emerged from the shelves of books, I was drawn to the opposite side of the store by the sight of the other, bright items stocked there: mugs and cards, sweatshirts and jogging shorts, stuffed animals and bumper stickers, jewelry and posters.

I wandered among them, touching them, trying to imagine what it would feel like to be a student, to be choosing which sweatshirt I would buy to wear to a basketball game.

I picked up a baby's T-shirt printed with CITY COLLEGE and a date twenty-one years in the future. I put my hand on my belly and felt the companionable rolling, like that of a little dolphin swimming inside me.

Would my baby look like the boy I had seen by the bookshelves, tall and muscular and handsome? Or like the cute redhead behind the cash register, whose curvy figure caused me a hard pinch of envy. Maybe my baby would look like the scrawny boy with heavy glasses and a big Adam's apple, going through the checkout line.

No. My baby would be beautiful.

I thought of what it would be like to be the mother of a college student. I wouldn't mind paying its tuition. I would send cookies and come for Parents' Weekend and cry at graduation.

I couldn't help thinking of Mama then, and of how happy she would have been to do those things for me. And how she'd never have the chance. I wondered what other things she might have wanted to do and wouldn't. She wouldn't because she'd quit making her own choices and had let Pop fashion her life for her.

And I was doing the same thing, I realized. Because I was afraid and uncertain, as Mama was, I was allowing T. Peter and Junior Lee and Mattie to propel me along. It was different with them than it was with Pop because they were good people who wanted to help, and some of the things they forced me into doing were things I should have done anyway. But they were still making my decisions, as I had allowed Scott to do, too, and that was dangerous. I didn't want to end up dependent and fearful like poor Mama.

I wondered why thinking about giving up something so dangerous should make me feel so bad.

I dropped the tiny T-shirt back on the shelf and ran out the door and down the steps to the bus stop.

The doctor opened my file and removed some papers. From across the desk, I couldn't see what they said, but I knew what they were.

"You're doing fine," he said. "For the next month, you'll be coming in every two weeks, and then once a week until delivery."

He turned the papers around so they faced me, and pushed them across the desk, placing a pen beside them.

"These are the relinquishment papers. The adoption can proceed much faster if they're signed before the birth. Some lucky couple will be getting a fine, healthy baby."

I looked at the papers but didn't take up the pen.

"Almost every young woman I see thinks at first

that she can raise a child alone," the doctor said.
"It usually takes a few months for her to see how
wrong she is. By then, the child has lost precious
time with its new family. Or the girl continues to
keep the baby and it's not good for either one of
them."

Still, I hesitated.

"Have you considered how much it costs to care
for a child properly? How much emotional effort is
involved?"

"I know," I said. "I have four little brothers."

"Then you also know this is the sensible thing.
This baby deserves a financially secure environ-
ment, with two parents to care for it. I'm sure you
want the best for your child."

"Yes, of course." But still I couldn't pick up the
pen.

The doctor sighed and leaned back in his chair.
"Daphne, I thought you'd already made this
decision."

"I have," I said, wiping damp palms on the knees
of my pants. "I'd just like to think of it as all mine
for a while longer, that's all."

He leaned forward again. "I urge you to do this
before the birth. Believe me, it'll be much easier for
you that way."

"I do believe you. Can't I wait two more weeks?
Until my next appointment?"

He sighed again and put the papers back in the
file. "If you wish."

Back at Mattie's, I went to my room to lie on my
beautiful quilt-covered bed for a rest before dinner.
I spread my hands over my stomach and felt the

baby—this baby I'd cared for and envied and sometimes hated for all the pain and loss it had caused me—and I knew I'd miss it when it was gone.

How I resented Scott's clean escape from all the consequences. He was in college, going to classes, having fun, free to go home for holidays, while I worked and worried and watched my stretch marks grow. Even after the baby was born and in its new home, I would have those marks. And others that couldn't be seen.

But that was the way it had to be and I'd better get used to it. And the baby wouldn't be my only loss. I'd have to leave Mattie and our peaceful meals, our gathering expeditions, our Sunday dinners with T. Peter and Junior Lee. I knew I had to start making my own plans, to get back in charge of myself. For all the effort I'd made to stay apart, somehow my life had twined with theirs and, dangerous as I knew that was, I had to admit I liked it. I even loved it.

# TWENTY-THREE

That night before dinner, I bathed my eyes in cold water and powdered around them, but I still looked as if I'd been crying.

Though Mattie would have had to be blind not to notice, I wasn't going to say anything unless she asked. I wasn't sure if I wanted her to or not.

At the dinner table, I tried to eat, but the food tasted like sawdust, and I couldn't swallow past the lump in my throat.

"Are you catching cold, Daphne?" Mattie asked me.

"No, I don't think so." I went back to stirring my soup.

"Don't you feel well?"

"I feel all right."

"Well, what's the matter?"

"Matter?"

"Come on, now. You might as well wear a sign that says I'VE BEEN CRYING. I thought you'd be all excited over the course catalogue you went to get this afternoon, and instead, you sit there looking like the end of the world. What happened?"

I thought I'd used up all the tears I had, when a fresh supply of them slid down my cheeks. I closed my eyes, but they kept coming.

Mattie came around to my chair and rested her hand on my shoulder. "You don't have to talk about it if you don't want to. It's none of my business. But it might help."

"I wish I could stop crying," I said. "I feel waterlogged."

"Go ahead and cry," Mattie said. "You're not doing it because it's so much fun. There's a reason. But let's get comfortable while you do it."

She led me into the living room and sat me down on one of the white couches. "I believe some wallowing is absolutely necessary. Nothing I hate more than sterling characters with permanent stiff upper lips." She sat beside me and waited.

Finally, I took a wad of damp tissues from my pocket and wiped my face. "I think I've wallowed enough."

"Anything special you're wallowing in?"

I couldn't tell her all of it—especially not how much I'd miss her.

"Just everything, I guess." I blew my nose. "You know, we only did it once. I ought to be in a textbook someplace. The Worst Case Scenario. I didn't even like it."

"Would you be crying less if you'd liked it more?" Mattie asked.

I had to laugh. "I suppose that's irrelevant, isn't it? But he got away with it, and I didn't."

"He got away with it because you let him. You could have told him."

"Why? He wasn't interested in anything serious with me. And this is about as serious as it can get."

"You didn't have to go ahead with the pregnancy."

"Even if I hadn't, I'd have paid a price he didn't have to."

"So, welcome to real life, my dear. You makes your choices, you takes your chances. Oh, I don't mean to sound so hard-hearted. My lack of graciousness shows up at the most awkward times." She patted my knee. "Do you regret those choices?"

"No. It would have been useless to tell him, and I couldn't have had an abortion. I'm sorry about the choice I made on prom night, though. I didn't think. I just wanted him to love me."

Mattie put her arm around me and rubbed my shoulder. "We're all hungry for that. Sometimes we're not wise in how we seek it, but it's a human failing. And we learn. I bet you won't make that kind of choice again."

"I certainly hope not." I could feel my chin trembling. "I'm tired of being so lumpy and ugly. You should have seen the girls on campus today, all slim and beautiful."

"Really, Daphne. Some of them must have had thick ankles and bad skin. Your condition, at least, is temporary. Anyway, T. Peter thinks you're the world's most perfect shape."

I laughed, a watery-sounding chuckle. Then I said, "My doctor's upset with me because I haven't signed the relinquishment papers yet."

"Why haven't you?"

"I'm not sure. I hate to think my baby"—I pressed my hands over my big stomach—"belongs to somebody else when it's still really mine. It's kept me company for so long, sometimes when I didn't have any other company. Oh, I know I'll have to do it, but I've already made so many hard decisions. This seems the hardest."

"Poor Daphne. What can I say? The rough stuff always seems to come in bunches. There's nothing for it but to put your head into the wind and keep going. That's all I've ever found to work."

My tears started up again as Mattie pulled me to her shoulder and patted my back.

# TWENTY-FOUR

T. Peter was standing at the door, ready to flip the sign from OPEN to CLOSED, when a tall thin girl with a nose as red as the muffler around her neck pushed it open.

"Hi," she said.

He looked at her for a moment, frowning. Then he said, "Noreen?"

"Yeah, it's me again."

"I thought you were in Montana." He flipped the sign. "We're just closing, but come in and have some coffee."

"Thanks." She rubbed her nose and sat at the counter.

I watched from the kitchen pass-through, irritated. I knew I wouldn't be able to work much longer, and I valued my lunches with T. Peter and Junior Lee too much to tolerate interruptions. I wouldn't even go out to help T. Peter. Maybe the girl would leave faster.

T. Peter poured coffee for Noreen and set the cup

in front of her. "What brings you back to town?"

"Montana," the girl said. "God, what a place. Miles and miles of nothing but miles and miles. The big excitement is going into town on Saturday night to drink at the Roundup. If it's a really rowdy crowd, they pour Wesson oil on the floor and dance."

"You didn't like it?" T. Peter asked.

Noreen laughed. "Not much. Some of the guests at the ranch were okay, but they were city folk. That's what I liked about them. So I figured I'd better get back to where everybody was city folk. Including me."

T. Peter leaned his elbows on the counter, listening.

She drank some coffee and put her cup down. "So I wondered if you still needed any help here."

T. Peter straightened up. "As a matter of fact, I might. I've got a terrific waitress now, but she's going to be taking some time off soon and I'll need a replacement. But the job's hers if she wants to come back. Just so you know that."

"Sounds okay. At least I'd have a chance to get situated again. When can I start?"

"I'll have to let you know. Where can I reach you?"

Noreen wrote a phone number on the back of a check she tore from T. Peter's pad, took another swallow of coffee, and got up. "Thanks. I'll be talking to you." She tightened her muffler as T. Peter unlocked the door for her, and she left.

I came out of the kitchen. "That which you are seeking is out there seeking you as well?" I asked.

"Looks that way," T. Peter answered, wiping the

counter. "At least when it comes to waitresses." He stopped wiping. "But I meant what I said. The job's yours whenever you want it."

"Thanks. But I'm not ready to quit yet."

"Well, it won't be long. You know, it's been quite a while since I delivered a baby, and I especially don't want to do it here."

This job was *mine*. And it was more than a job. It was lunches with T. Peter and Junior Lee, joking with the regulars, my own mug on the rack—home.

And it was one more thing I'd have to give up.

Once Noreen took my place, I might never get it back, no matter what T. Peter said. It was impossible to know how the future would unfold; there were booby traps all along the way.

T. Peter put his arm around my shoulders. "You're destined for better things than waitressing, anyway, and we both know it. Besides, there's still Sunday dinner at Mattie's."

It sounded as if he were preparing me for not ever coming back to the Gourmaniac. And for how many more Sundays would there be dinner at Mattie's?

T. Peter lifted my chin with his finger. "Why such a tragic look? Nothing's going to spoil our friendship, don't you know that? Even if I didn't see you for years, I'd still be your friend."

Once again, the tears I was so sick of misted my eyes.

"Years?" I asked. He nodded.

On the next-to-last Sunday in January, T. Peter and Junior Lee arrived at Mattie's with dinner and gift-wrapped packages.

A chocolate cake with eighteen candles sat in the middle of Mattie's dining-room table, and when it was time for me to blow them out, I had to hold my stomach to keep it out of the frosting.

"We'd have had a party to mark your last week at work anyway," Mattie said, handing me a package. "Just a lucky coincidence it's your birthday, too."

I didn't think it was lucky. I was losing a job and a year, all at once. I had no control over the year, but I'd been the one to decide when to quit my job.

With only a few weeks to go until the baby came, I was too slow and awkward to be the kind of fast, nimble waitress the Gourmaniac needed. Also, being on my feet so long made my legs ache, my ankles swell, and my stomach muscles feel as if they were ready to surrender to gravity. I was afraid I'd suddenly find my massive midsection somewhere around my knees.

"You're a legal adult now," Junior Lee told me, putting another package in my hands. "You can vote and go to war, but you can't drink alcohol in this state. Makes no sense to me, but nobody ever asked me."

"And they're not likely to," T. Peter said, piling on a third present.

I opened my gifts: books, records, a nightgown. Nothing for a baby, nothing even to suggest a baby existed. I hadn't expected anything of the sort, but still it made me sad. Having this baby was a life-changing event for me, and yet, as soon as it was born, I'd have to go on as if nothing had ever happened.

Just two days before, I'd been unable, once again, to sign the relinquishment papers.

The days that followed were long and empty. Without the Gourmaniac, I could sleep later, but now I was too enormously pregnant to be able to sleep well. Junior Lee would have called that irony, I supposed.

When Mattie went gathering, she went alone, feeling I would be safer and more comfortable at home than on the back of a motorbike, out in the cold. Then I drifted through the quiet, neat house, looking at Mattie's pictures, standing in the doorway of my pretty room, memorizing it, sitting on the white couch, staring into the fire. Every afternoon, I took a long walk in the frosty air, killing time until Mattie returned and I could examine the day's treasures from the saddlebags.

On the last day of January, I came home from my walk to find Mattie sitting at the dining-room table, a glass of wine in front of her, her face in her hands.

"What is it?" I asked.

Mattie's shoulders shook, and I went to stand behind her. Cautiously, I raised my hands until they rested on Mattie's back. "Can you tell me?"

"I came home early," Mattie said, her voice choked and muffled. "It was so cold, all I could think of was a bowl of popcorn in front of the fire. When I opened the door, I heard the phone ringing, but I thought you were here. It kept ringing, though, so I ran for it, and it was William."

"William?" I asked, rubbing Mattie's shoulders. "Are he and Geneva in town?"

"No, no. He said Geneva was tired this morning,

so she lay down for a rest after breakfast. And when he went to wake her, he couldn't. It must have been a stroke."

"You mean she's . . ." My hands stilled.

"She's dead." Mattie sounded amazed.

"Oh, Mattie. I'm so sorry." I put my arms all the way around Mattie and held her, my bulging stomach pressing into the back of the chair. I couldn't understand why, for all my recent susceptibility to tears, my eyes were dry, but I was glad.

It was my turn to offer help. "When are you going?"

"Going?"

"Aren't you going to help William? With the . . . arrangements?"

"I hadn't thought . . ."

I hugged her. She seemed so dazed and uncertain, so unlike Mattie. "You have to go. She was your sister, your family. I'll watch everything. Don't worry."

Mattie patted my hands and raised her head. "Of course, I have to go. Only for a few days."

I loosened my arms. "Can I help you pack? Or anything?"

"I'll be all right." She straightened her back. "Would you keep me company while I get ready?"

Mattie left early the next morning, by taxi, for the airport. The day stretched before me, blank and silent.

I was half an hour early for my one o'clock appointment at the clinic, and I found a kind of companionship, sitting in the hard wooden waiting-room chair, surrounded by other women and their children. After my appointment, during which my doctor made no effort to hide his impatience with my failure to sign the papers, I stood on the sidewalk, dreading the return to Mattie's lonely house.

Instead of getting on the bus that would take me there, I boarded the next one that came along, one that would let me off near the Gourmaniac.

It was almost two-thirty when I reached Eighth Avenue, and I wondered if Noreen now stayed for lunch, the way I used to. I didn't think I could stand to know that Noreen shared that time, too.

I hesitated a moment before opening the door. Perhaps I should have gone on back to Mattie's. But it was too cold to stand out there thinking about that, and the inside of the Gourmaniac looked so warm and welcoming.

As soon as I was through the door, T. Peter came running across the room and hugged me. "Daphne!" he cried. "Just who I've been needing to see all day."

I hugged him back.

"And just in time for lunch. We've missed you."

"Does . . . does Noreen stay for lunch now?" I asked.

"No, no, no," T. Peter said. "I don't even think Noreen eats at all. I haven't seen a bonier body since the skeleton we used for orthopedics in medical school. Anyway," he whispered in my ear, "we don't want her to. We're saving your chair for you."

That warmed me more than coming in from the cold street.

He flipped the sign to CLOSED, locked the door, and took me to a table. "Junior Lee," he called, "look who's here."

Junior Lee came out of the kitchen with my mug full of hot chocolate and presented it to me. Then he dropped into the chair opposite me. "I'm done. Your turn, chief."

Noreen appeared, buttoning her coat and winding her long red scarf around her neck. "Bye, guys. See you tomorrow." And she was out the door.

"How's she doing?" I asked.

"Oh, she's okay," Junior Lee said, as T. Peter headed for the kitchen. "She hasn't got your hustle, but she's not as bad as some. I sure am tired of listening to what a lousy place Montana is, though. I've got a mind to take a look at it myself to see if it can possibly be that bad. So how's Miss Mattie doing?"

"She's gone for a few days. Her sister died, and she went to the funeral."

"Is she okay?"

"Well, naturally she's sad. I don't think they were very close. They hadn't seen each other in a long time, but Geneva was the only one left besides Mattie of all the brothers and sisters. And once Mattie was in love with her sister's husband." As soon as I said it, I wished I hadn't. Mattie hadn't said it was a secret, but maybe it was.

"Poor Miss Mattie," Junior Lee said. "Probably having some complicated feelings about now."

T. Peter came out of the kitchen with lunch, and I told him, too, about Geneva. He looked at me and said, "You okay there by yourself? One of us could come stay with you."

"I'm fine," I said. "Mattie'll be home day after tomorrow. But I wouldn't mind if you came for supper tomorrow."

They did, bringing enough food so there'd be leftovers for Mattie's first dinner home. As valuable as their company always was, it was still more so after a single whole day all alone.

"How was it?" I asked the next day, taking Mattie's coat and hanging it up.

"Sad, as you'd expect," Mattie said, looking unfamiliar in a plain gray suit. "Let me go change, and I'll tell you."

When Mattie returned in slacks and a sweater, I had a pot of tea and T. Peter's chocolate pie on the coffee table in front of the fire.

"Oh, lovely," Mattie said. "There's no place I like as much as my own house." She poured herself a cup of tea. "I'm glad I went. William and I cried together, but he'll feel the loss more than I. He really loved her. When he chose her instead of me, it was the right thing." She sipped her tea and stared into the fire. "It's so strange. We weren't close, but at least I always knew she was there, my only family. Now she's gone."

# TWENTY-FIVE

On the first Friday after Mattie got back, she and I sat in the kitchen, eating BLTs that I had made and chili from a can.

"I've got to take some of my new things in to Vivian this afternoon," Mattie said. "Will you be okay here alone?"

"Sure," I said. "Why not?"

"Well, it's getting close to the time for the baby."

"It's still over three weeks away. I went to the clinic while you were gone, and the doctor said everything was normal."

"I'm getting nervous, I guess."

"You can't be more nervous than I am."

"Daphne, have you signed those papers yet?"

I shook my head slowly. "I lie in bed at night and feel the baby turning inside me, and I think how much I love that feeling. It's so strange. I thought I'd die when I found out I was pregnant and now I hate to think of it being over. In one of your old novels, I read about a pregnant woman who said she carried her little one under her heart. That's exactly how I feel. I even feel as if there's a connection from my heart to the baby. And after it's born, that connection will still be there, no matter where the baby goes."

Mattie reached out and touched my hand. "I can go to Vivian's tomorrow."

"I'm okay. You go ahead. I'll take a walk, and then come back and have a nap. Don't worry."

"Well, bundle up good."

"That's impossible. Nothing will close over my stomach anymore."

After Mattie had left for the gallery, in a cab to accommodate all her pictures, I stretched a sweater over my stomach, put on my gloves, ski jacket, and earmuffs, and locked the door behind me.

I stood on the front porch, rubbing my back with my gloved hands and wondering why Mother Nature had designed things so inefficiently. Anybody could tell you that carrying a baby, or anything else, stuck out in front like this was the worst possible thing for your back. It would be much easier to carry a baby between your shoulder blades, like a backpack. It wouldn't be in the way all the time, you could sleep on your stomach, and there wouldn't be any heartburn or going to the bathroom every half hour. I wondered if Mother Nature was really a man. Surely, a woman would have thought of these things.

Yet, as inconvenient and uncomfortable as being pregnant was, my pregnancy was what linked me to three people I loved. Four, if I counted the baby. It had become impossible for me to resent the little person who, though it had cost me so much, had brought me to Mattie, T. Peter, and Junior Lee.

Even though T. Peter had promised me his friendship for years to come, I believed it was the temporary urgency of the coming baby that really kept him with me, and that, without it, our connection would fade. I was an emergency they had all rallied to, an emergency that would be ending soon.

I didn't see how I could go back to working at the Gourmaniac after I left Mattie's. It would remind me of too much. I was sure now I could take care of myself. I had some money. I knew how to enroll in college, to find another place to live, another job. What I didn't know was how to do without them all. And I was certain that I'd never again be so tough that being without them didn't hurt.

As I started down the porch steps, I felt something warm and wet gushing down the insides of my legs. Had that inconsiderate child kicked me in the bladder again? Now I'd have to go back into the house, take off all my layers, and begin over. Turning back to remount the steps, I felt a tugging sensation across my stomach and an answering pressure in my back.

"Oh, my God," I said out loud. "My water's broken."

The ending had begun. I wanted to weep.

Hurrying now, I unlocked the door and went to my room to change. I didn't know how much time I had, but as I pulled on dry clothes, I decided not to wait for Mattie. Nothing could be allowed to go wrong now, not after all the care I'd taken of this baby so far. Even if its arrival meant the end of my own recent happiness, there was nothing I could do but finish well what I'd started so heedlessly.

From the phone in the kitchen I called my doctor, who told me he'd meet me at the hospital. Then I called a cab. I looked at my watch: just two o'clock.

I dialed again, and when T. Peter answered the phone, I said, "How'd you like to have lunch at the hospital?"

"Daphne?" he yelled. "Is this it?"

"Looks that way. And Mattie's on her way to the gallery, so I've called a cab. Can you reach her there and tell her what's going on? I've got to pack my bag."

"Right, right. Of course. Don't worry about a thing. We'll be there as fast as we can. And, honey"—he paused—"we love you."

"Me, too. See you later."

I flew to my room, massaging the ache in my back, to get packed before the cab arrived. Rummaging through my drawers for a nightgown, underwear, and other essentials, I uncovered the slim packet of Scott's letters, then shoved them back under my folded clothes.

I zipped up my bag and headed for the front door. The cab should be here any minute. With my fingers an inch from the doorknob, I dropped the bag and ran clumsily back to my room. I jerked open the top drawer of my dresser, pawed through the contents until I found Scott's letters, and carried them to the kitchen. After I'd ripped them into quarters and thrown them into the garbage can, I thought, I hope it never occurs to Mattie to go through her own trash.

\* \* \*

The cab driver seemed unconcerned when I told him I was having a baby.

"I've got five kids, sis, and every one of them took all night getting here. We've got lots of time."

I wasn't so sure. The contractions were strong, and with each one I could feel the muscles of my stomach harden and rise almost to a point. As each contraction subsided, I gasped for air, realizing I'd held my breath for its duration.

We finally reached the hospital emergency room, but the driver had to wait for a contraction to finish before I could pay him and get out.

"Good luck, sis," he said, getting back into the driver's seat. "Lucky thing they're worth all the trouble they cause."

I waddled into the reception area, where a nurse took one look at my face and ran for a wheelchair. Then someone else stuck a clipboard full of admission forms into my hands, whipped it away as soon as I'd filled them out, and the wheelchair was off, rolling down the corridor.

Mama always said she forgot the hurtful parts of having a baby as soon as it arrived, that the effort was worth the reward. During that long afternoon and evening, I was sure I'd never forget the feeling of being torn apart by that primal struggle.

The doctor kept saying that everything was proceeding normally, but I didn't see how something that felt so awful could be normal. The shots of Demerol I got made me so groggy that I fell asleep between contractions, but each new pain woke me with a shock.

Mattie and T. Peter each came in once to see me.

They'd left Junior Lee in the waiting room, they said, because he was in worse shape than I was. He only liked things hard when they were happening to him. He couldn't stand having hard things happen to someone else.

They held my hands and gave me ice to suck, but I didn't want them to stay. It was too difficult to be brave for them, not just about the pain of labor, but about the pain of losing them when the labor was over.

Eventually, I didn't care about anything except getting the baby out. Just then, I couldn't think about two painful things at once.

The doctor came in to check me for what seemed like the millionth time and yelled, "Okay, let's go!"

He ran out of the room, as two nurses grabbed the ends of my bed and pushed it down the hall and through a set of swinging doors. I felt light-headed and furious. What was this baby doing to me, after all the care I'd taken of it? It had messed up my life once, in Seeley, and now it was about to do it again, in Lincoln. I couldn't wait to get rid of it.

The delivery room was too bright. Lights glittered off tile and steel and illuminated the creases in acres of green cloth.

"Come on, come on, push, push, push," the doctor kept saying, and I tried to do what he said.

Suddenly there was a little baby lying on my deflated stomach.

I laughed out loud. Mama was right.

She was beautiful. Wisps of wet, silvery hair lay against her head, and she stared at me with big dark eyes, her little fists clenched under her chin.

"Isn't she supposed to cry?" I asked, touching her with one finger.

"She's okay," the doctor said. "She'll do plenty of that later."

"Hi, sweetheart," I whispered, and burst into tears, knowing that someone else would hear all her cries.

# TWENTY-SIX

There was a nighttime hush in the hospital as I lay in bed, my face pressed into the pillow to keep my sobs from waking my roommates.

All it had taken was the first glimpse of my silvery-haired little girl for me to know I had to sign the relinquishment papers as soon as possible. Whatever fantasies I'd had about keeping her disappeared. This baby had to have all the things I alone couldn't give her.

I pressed my face harder into the pillow as I wondered who could ever love her as much as I already did.

A sliver of light fell into the room as the door opened, and I heard a cross voice saying, "Only for a few minutes. This is very irregular."

Three shadows came to my bedside. One of them quietly pulled the curtain around the bed, and another switched on the dim wall light.

Mattie sat by my bed and wiped my tears with the edge of the sheet. "Don't cry. Please don't cry."

I took Mattie's hand. "Did you see her?" I whispered, still tearful.

"Yes," T. Peter whispered back. "We just had a peek at her down in the nursery. She's beautiful."

I nodded, unable to speak.

Junior Lee was just as silent until T. Peter poked him in the side and said, "Say something."

Junior Lee cleared his throat, but that was the only sound he could produce.

"Oh, well," T. Peter reminded me, "you know how strong emotion shuts him up."

"I wish it would shut me up," I said. "I feel like I'm going to cry forever."

Mattie took my hand in both of hers. "Maybe not. Listen, Daphne. Are you listening to me? We had dinner together, T. Peter and Junior Lee and me. And we discovered we'd all been thinking the same thing and wondering how we could make it happen. We don't want you to give up our baby."

"Your baby?"

"We care about her as much as we care about you. We want to help you raise her. We're willing to do it legally if you want: become guardians, draw up documents, whatever it takes."

"What?"

"You both can live with me. You can all live with me if you want. Please, Daphne. I've never had a baby. I've never had a family of my own. I want one now."

The tears stopped. I was too stunned to cry. "But what about your work? Your peace and privacy?"

"I've had enough of that to last me forever. I want some life now. Junior Lee's right. You can have more than one spot of red. I'm unbalanced with only one. I don't want to end up emotionless, like those love letters of Michelle's. Please say yes."

"Please say yes," T. Peter said. "I want to know her the way I didn't know my boys."

Junior Lee found his voice. "Please say yes. I've always wanted to be a big brother. Think of the trouble I can get her into."

I heard the echo of Mattie's words about doing whatever it took so we could all stay together, and finally understood that love doesn't have an artificial limit of time or distance or place, or even of blood. It goes on as long as everyone involved is willing to do whatever it takes to keep it going. Scott didn't want to do that, or Pop, but Mattie and T. Peter and Junior Lee and I did. And Mama, too. It was hard for me to believe that these were people I'd once been afraid to depend on. Not anymore. Love meant I could.

Light from the night lamp splintered through my tears into bright fragments, like a tossed handful of confetti.

# TWENTY-SEVEN

I sat with Junior Lee on the white couch, the baby asleep on my knees. One of her tiny hands was curled around his finger. I'd never seen him sit so still for so long.

Together we watched as T. Peter helped Mattie hang a new picture over the fireplace.

On the coffee table lay the note I had just received from Mama, a note written in response to my own. My letter was meant only for her, to tell her of her granddaughter, and of our new life, but I didn't really care if Pop read it, too. What he thought now didn't matter at all.

Mama's few lines told more than the words alone: they spoke of forgiveness, of joy and pain, and, most of all, of future hopes.

Dear Daphne,

Thank you for telling me about the baby. She'll be our secret. And thank you for making my name her middle name. It rests my heart to know how well things have worked out for you. I know I'll see you and Holly Marie one day, so until then, all my love to all of you.

Mama

I, too, knew we would see each other again one day. Maybe not until I finished college, but the right time would come. Holly was a gift I wanted to share with Mama, and perhaps, eventually, with the boys. But never, never with Pop. Whom I chose to have in my life was even more important now that I had Holly to think of.

"Ta-da," T. Peter said, coming down from the step stool and gesturing with both hands to the newly hung picture.

It was one of Mattie's collages. As always, the canvas was heaped with her gatherings, but all of them, instead of being painted white, had been smartened up with fresh bright colors, so they looked brand-new. In the center, a red circle outlined five small dolls: two male, two female, and a pink baby.

Across the bottom were Mattie's initials and the words *Home: No. 1.*